Emerald Dreams

Unless otherwise stated Scriptures quoted here are from the King James Version (Authorised version). First published in 1611. Quoted from the KJV Classic Reference Bible, copyright 1983 by the Zondervan Corporation.

Published by: Reading Stones Publishing.
Helen Brown & Wendy Wood

Cover Design: Wendy Wood
Photo Credits:
Models Photo: Carpe Noctem Photography; Jennifer Maybury
Stock images from Shutterstock, used with permission.

For more copies contact the Publisher at:

Glenburnie Homestead
212 Glenburnie Road
ROB ROY NSW 2360
Mobile: 0422 577 663
Email: hbrown19561@gmail.com

Gems of Australia
Faith Series
Book 3

Emerald Dreams

Olwyn Harris

Dedication: For Grandma Elvie
who gave wings to my dreams,
especially writing…

My heartfelt appreciation to Noelene Dempsey:
Thanks for your wisdom in verifying references to
Indigenous culture & customs.

1.

The bus pulled over in a swirl of dust in the car park. It was deserted, with the exception of one lonely campervan on the other side of the camping grounds. A retired couple were sipping tea and looking at the thick canopy of trees through binoculars. Andi could see the lady flicking her way through a pocket-sized book and reading bits to the man who munched contentedly on a biscuit, still looking steadfastly at the leaves. Suddenly his wife pointed excitedly past the greenery into the open sky. He handed over the glasses to his wife. There, far above the canopy, gliding on air currents was a wedged tail eagle. The diamond shape of its tail fanned out like an enormous rudder, the feathers on the tips of its huge wings separated in little fingers and curled up ever so slightly. Around and around, using the air to soar. The woman put her book down. Her husband sat back in his chair as she joined him quietly finishing their tea, enjoying the moment with a sigh.

"Did you see that?" said Andi, catching her breath as she watched the eagle circle out of sight. It reminded her of her life with God. Using the currents was like the flow of God's strength to soar higher. She could use that for their devotion tonight. The doors opened, a bursting dam of eleven and twelve-year-old kids as they ran off the bus, running wild around the park. "Eagles are awesome," she said half to herself, flicking her funky haircut. She had her hair done for this trip. She even dyed it green across the fringe. The reaction from the girls was worth it. They loved it.

Jo nodded. This weekend was about encountering nature. Imagine meeting a koala, an echidna, or a platypus. Wouldn't it be great to see something like that in the wild? The couple stood up and put away their binoculars, waving at the bus as it emptied its cargo. Their bird watching moments were suspended for now. Now they were on duty. They came over and introduced themselves as Mr and Mrs Hollis, their Camp Grandparents.

While the kids were tearing around letting off steam, Jo and Andi joined the other team-leader 'Buddies' and were given a quick brief by their Adventure Club leader, Scott Hamlin. He was tall, athletic and had a gifted way with kids. A whistle and a holler and the kids gradually assembled around him. "Quiet everyone. We're going to pray before we start. "Heavenly Father, thank you for keeping us safe on our trip. Thank you for everyone on this adventure and for Your awesome creation. Help us to understand a bit more about how much you love us, by the time we're ready to go home. We ask for your protection while we are here. Amen."

He looked up and smiled. "Now, you all know your teams. Has anyone *not* figured out the colour of their activity folder yet?" There were some sniggers as Scott good-naturedly gave his run down of the afternoon. "Mr and Mrs Hollis are Adventure Camp Grandparents – so you can talk to them about anything that's bothering you. Hands up those boys in the Red group…" and he proceeded to allocate camp duties to each of the coloured teams. "Miss Jo and Miss Andi are the

Green Team Buddies. You'll be setting up your camp and getting tea started. Everyone pitches in. We need to be done before dusk – we have a Ranger from the National Parks and Wildlife Service coming to meet us at 7.30 to take us on our first night walk. Hopefully we'll get to see some really cool nocturnal animals. Any questions?" He answered the predictable sort of queries: 'Where's the toilet?'; 'When do we eat?'; and 'Are there snakes?'; and then he dismissed them to their duties.

Jo had been really looking forward to this weekend. Her enthusiasm for the Adventure Club was infectious, and the girls loved her. She picked up some sleeping bags and started carrying them over to where the others had dumped their tent. She dropped the bags on the ground. "I'm so glad you've come Andi. I know camping under *canvas* is a big ask!"

Andi shrugged and pulled out the diagram on how to erect the tent. "I figured that even if I don't sleep a wink – it's only a few days. Besides the girls are great." Their Green Team was Josie, Sarah, Abby, and Lauren. "Are you ready Girls? We're going to put up our Green canvas palace. Where is north? We need to face the tent so we will be in the shade all afternoon. West is… let me see…" She stared her compass.

"Why don't we just put it in the shade? Its already afternoon. The sun could well be in the same place this time tomorrow… don't you think?" Jo laughed at Andi's serious study of the pamphlet. Jo was delightedly surprised at Andi's willingness to be involved in this weekend. Andi was usually an inside sort of girl. She winked at the girls and said very quietly… "She doesn't do much of this getting-back-to-nature stuff! She's going to need our help."

As Andi was in the process of studying the pamphlet, Jo had Abbey, Josie and Sarah drag the canvas bundle over into the shade and start hammering their tent pegs in place. Andi looked up from her diagram in amazement as their tent was already miraculously assembled. A little tension on a couple of guy-ropes and they were finished.

"How did you *do* that?"

"Camping Badge practice. Being first up should be worth some points! Quick girls – we need to roll out our beds and show these boys how camping is done!"

* * *

Scott stood and introduced "Ranger Dave" to the campers who stood in a clump shining their torches in each other's eyes. "We'll need to be quiet, so we don't scare off the animals."

"Righto," said Dave brightly, "Let's get walking. Stay close so we don't get separated and you can hear what I'm saying." He strode out and along the walking track, followed by the campers sounding very much like a herd of wild buffalo stampeding through the bush. Their flashing torches resembled a laser light show, warning every creature that tonight *campers* were out and about.

Dave paused. "I want your groups to stand in a circle." Everyone repositioned, shuffling around in the dark with a fair share of jabs and stepping on toes. "Now," said Dave in even, controlled tones; he had obviously done this before. "Be very quiet." A few giggles from the girls trickled around the edges as the groups hushed. One of the boys ran a stick down Sarah's arm and she let out a terrified squeal. Boys sniggered; high fives given in appreciation.

"Now," said Ranger Dave very firmly, "I want you to turn off your torches." One or two kids gasped. Abby hung on tightly to Andi's hand.

"If you look up you will see the stars through the canopy. Well, okay – no stars tonight because of the cloud cover. I want you to listen very carefully though."

"It's so quiet," said one of the girls. A boy burped, and spontaneous giggles erupted again.

"When you hear something that is *not* your neighbour, tell me what you think it might be…" And the quietness resumed.

"I can hear wind in the leaves…" said someone.

"I can hear a frog…" offered someone else.

"That was Jason. There ain't no frogs," his partner objected.

There was a pause. "Mo-poke, mo-poke…." said another.

"That's the call of a Boobook Owl. What some people call a "Mopoke" is actually a tawny frogmouth and its call is quite different. See if you can hear one…it's more like a drum… Kinda like: 'Oom, Oom, Oom'."

"I can hear … a dog…"

"Well done… that dog is actually a Barking Owl. There are old stories of kids getting lost in the bush at night because they went out looking for their dog. There are birds called Bush thick-knees or bush stone-curlews that make a rather blood-curdling scream… and you can imagine what sort of stories grew out of that… particularly in the early days when people were straight from Europe. They had never heard the kinds of sounds our native Australian birds and animals make before. To them the bush was a dark, scary, unfriendly place."

"Thanks for that Ranger Dave," muttered Andi.

A boy made an exaggerated choking, gasping sound and Abby started to whimper. Jo could feel Josie trembling, and she put her arm around her shoulders. "Righto – turn your torches on," said Dave in a very practical voice, "but shine them up in the leaves… be very quiet and you might see a possum. Look in the forks of the branches."

Sarah turned around and came face to face with the contorted expression of a face illuminated by a torch held close under the chin, grotesquely moaning. She squealed. Josie saw it at the same time out of the corner of her eye, shrieking in terror. Abby joined in the frenzied vent of horror. Lauren knocked the torch out of the practical joker's hand and told him off for being "a beastly idiot". His team-mate defended his honour, congratulating him on the resounding success of the prank.

It was getting out of hand. Jo gathered the girls in her arms and looked to Scott for assistance through the dark. He cleared his throat quietly, his inexperience with nightlight shows evident. "Boys – cut it out. Girls, there's nothing to be afraid of. We can't go on until you're all settled."

"Can't go on anyway," whispered Sarah. "I can't! I want to go home…"

Jo held her tightly reassuring. "I'm right here…"

"I don't want to stay either…"

Andi looked to Scott and shook her head. "Can we take them back to camp? We'll get them some supper and settle them for bed. Maybe they can do the walk tomorrow night."

Under the circumstances, it seemed the wisest course of action. "Fair enough, we'll see you at suppertime."

Jo brightly took the girls by their hand and steered them back towards camp. "Do you want to know something? I have a secret and illegal stash of goodies in my bag. I was going to save them for a mid-night picnic… but I reckon a special supper might be in order *tonight*! We've had enough frights for one night. Girls, we need to spoil ourselves!"

Lauren agreed wholeheartedly. Josie giggled. "You? You weren't even scared…"

"Yeah, but I could've been…"

"We stick together. We get scared together; we feast together. That's the rule!" They flashed their torches along the path and soon the glow of the campsite was welcoming them back.

They sat around the campfire as Mr Hollis toasted some marshmallows. Mrs Hollis did a second round of chocolaty, milky Milo drinks. Jo broke out some potato chips and passed around some chocolate-frogs. They had a regular party. "I don't suppose you're ready for bed, hey Girls?" Jo said presently.

Abby shivered involuntarily. "Nah. I just want to sit here," she said as she snuggled deeper into Mrs Hollis' warm-hearted, ample frame. Sarah was sitting on the other side of Mrs Hollis, her nose deep in another mug of Milo.

"I'm okay," said Josie determinedly, as she passed Mr Hollis another marshmallow to skewer onto his toasting stick. Lauren had a mouth full of sticky marshmallow and mumbled something through the goo.

"If you want to retire, you can. These young ladies are just fine with us," offered Mrs Hollis.

"Retire? Oh no. I don't want to go to bed…." said Jo quickly. "I was hoping to catch the last of the night walk. We might get to see something interesting."

Mr Hollis laughed in a jovial, good-natured way. "I'd be surprised if they see so much as a possum. We'll probably see more here." He signalled to the girls and pointed to the base of a tree near the boys' tent. Two large, bright eyes twinkled. He sniffed around cautiously with his whiskered little nose… and then ran around the tree, its thick bushy tail following behind. "My guess is you'd be better to get up early and go down by the creek, just on dawn. You see all sorts of things at that time of day…"

He saw Jo's look of disappointment. "Still, if you're keen," he continued, "you just never know what you might see *tonight*. They were going along the old Pioneers Circuit… so if you turn left, you'll meet them coming back. Watch the stairs near the creek though. They get slippery."

Jo brightened instantly. "Well, I wouldn't mind going for the walk. We'll go down to the creek in the morning too. This is a gorgeous spot."

Andi extracted a bag of jelly-snakes from her backpack. She ripped open the bag and handed them around. She pocketed a few as well. "Energy food…" she said with a grin. "We'll be back to finish supper with the others."

* * *

2.

They followed the track along, enjoying the night quiet. "I can't believe those boys. You should suggest they have separate night hikes. Would be simpler," said Andi with a sigh.

"Yeah well, boys will be boys."

Andi shook her head. "There are times and places, and a moonless night in the middle of nowhere, is not one of them!" She flashed her torch over the sign that described the circuit." She took a deep breath. Underneath the canopy of forest trees, the air seemed even muggier. "Mr Hollis said we would meet the others if we took the left track."

"But then we won't get much of a walk! It's a circuit, so I guarantee we'll catch them up. You saw how much progress they were making. They're probably not even halfway yet."

"I don't know… maybe we should…"

"Come on," said Jo impatiently. "Let's get going or they'll catch us up and we won't get a walk at all." They turned right, shrouded in darkness as they walked along. There was silence except for the quiet fall of their feet on the leafy track. Nothing moved. Jo shone her torch up over the giant trees. "Maybe there is not a native animal left within the whole reserve," she said. "This silence is eerie."

"Don't you start! But I do love a good conspiracy theory." Andi paused dramatically. "Perhaps we could expose the cover-up. Imagine the news reports:" She laughed and assumed her best correspondent's voice, "Nature trekkers expose wildlife conspiracy! All native Australian animals have been extinct for years. There are no new photographs since the last world war. Supposed native animal photos are actually digitally remastered to look original."

"and…" continued Jo, "further investigations reveal that film footage of our unique native fauna are high-resolution computer generated images!"

"And…oh, look! Shhh! Over there! That's some CGI." Andi's torch flashed on the iridescent reflection of bright nocturnal eyes.

"A possum!" Jo adjusted her light. Her voice dropped to a whisper. "He's so cute! His tail looks like a hairbrush."

"Sshh! She a mother! She's carrying a little baby on her back! How cute is that? I didn't know possums did that – like koalas… wow…"

"There's two! *Twin* babies!" Jo's voice was low and excited. She followed the amazing sight with her torch as the mother struggled along the branch with her heavy burden. "What are baby possums called – kittens, cubs, pups…?"

"Joeys, I think," said Andi. The girls picked their way carefully around a fallen branch watching with mesmerised focus the little miracle before them. They hardly dared to breathe in case it evaporated in front of their eyes.

"Free loaders. I wonder if these kids ever give their mother a break?" Jo sighed as the mother disappeared into the hollow of a tree.

They heard another scuffle of leaves and shone their torches towards the sound. Stock still, they didn't move as a little pointy nose poked out from behind a root. His oversized ears wobbled sensitively. "Bandicoot," whispered Andi amazed.

He sniffed the ground squeaking as he nosed around busily. The girls quietly followed him in the torchlight as he shuffled along foraging industriously.

"I like him. He's really adorable. We're lucky in Australia… lots of endearing furry animals," surmised Andi quietly.

"An enormous grizzly bear would be exciting," offered Jo. "Although we do have a rather exclusive collection of the most venomous reptiles in the world."

"Gee – I *really* needed to be reminded of that just now," said Andi flashing the torch on the ground in front of her.

The bandicoot heard them then, pricked up his ears, alert. He scuttled under a low fallen branch and disappeared.

Jo sighed a long, satisfied sigh. "That was sooo worth it! They boys can bully us for the rest of the weekend now and I won't mind a bit!"

"Well, I'm keen for supper," said Andi. "Perhaps we should go straight back, and not worry about trying to meet up with the group. I can hear some roasted marshmallows calling my name."

The girls looked up and shone the torch around. They stood unable to say anything. Suddenly every tree looked the same. Andi covered her mouth with her hand. Her lip began an uncontrollable tremble.

"Well, the walking-track can't be far. We've only been off it for a second," said Jo hesitantly.

"We shouldn't have gone off it at all. We know that. I *know* that! How completely stupid! I can't believe we did that. What if the girls were with us?"

"Well, one – they're not. And two, we wouldn't have, if they were. And three – beating ourselves up is not going to help." Jo spoke in dot-points when she was stressed. "Now, let's just take a deep breath and we'll just retrace our steps. Like I said, it can't be far." She purposefully turned around to get her bearings and picked her way back over the large roots of a spreading tree.

They went on for a while before Andi pulled her to a stop. "Jo, we could be just going further away from the track. There is no way to tell. What are we going to do?" She shivered, the rising panic in her chest catching on the words as she spoke.

"Well…" Jo shone her torch over the ground. The little spot of light seemed ridiculously diminished in the enormity of their predicament.

"Oh. Jo, I'm getting really scared…"

Jo tried to say something, but she couldn't form the words. "Yeah. Me too," she conceded.

They sat down in the warm, forest damp and shivered from the fear that stole over their hearts. Something screeched long and high in the trees and Andi jumped, her jittery nerves strung tight like a violin string.

"Staying in one spot is supposed to be a good thing to do… when you're lo…" Andi couldn't finish. Saying the word was more than admitting a stupid mistake; it was too final. She had to pray. "Oh God… you know where we are. And… and

I'm really sorry… we should never have gone off the track. But, please… can you send some help?"

"And keep us from losing it while we are waiting," added Jo quietly.

"Well, if the worst comes to worse… we just wait until morning when we can see better. That's been done before. Not ideal, but we'll just be a little bit damp and a big bit hungry." Jo was trying really hard to play it all down.

Andi pulled the long, coloured lolly-snakes from her trackpants, sticky from the heat so that fluff from her pocket made them kind of furry. "Here," she said as she passed half to Jo. "It's just that it seems like a big deal, at the moment." Andi brightened momentarily. "What if we listen really carefully? We'll sure to hear the boys walking past… they certainly made enough noise… then we can call out…"

"Maybe. Except that we went the other way… they have already gone over this part of the walking track."

"Oh." Andi shivered in close to her friend's arm. "What was that?" The silence of the bush suddenly seemed alive with an orchestra of noises they had never heard before; and every one was a malicious dark reminder that hectares and hectares of lonely Australian bush surrounded them.

* * *

A gust of wind whistled around the trees, blowing leaf litter up in eddies against their faces. The girls shivered and huddled together. A grumble of thunder echoed around the hills and gullies. Jo turned off their torch to save the batteries. The inky darkness was broken as lightening flashed overhead, growling as it lit up the black canopy above them like an eerie

20

stroboscope. Suddenly they became aware of a low, sinister roar in the distance. "What is that noise? Thunder?"

"It's not just thunder," said Andi.

Jo jumped to her feet and flicked on the torch. "Quick, let's go!" She flashed the torch around. Great trees stood moaning as the wind became stronger and the rumble became louder like the crash of surf.

"But… I thought we were to…"

"Where?" muttered Jo under breath flashing her torch around. "Oh God help us!"

"Jo!"

"Andi stay with me. We have to find shelter… quick!"

Andi stood stock still, frozen. "We are in the middle of no-where!" she said anxiously.

Jo grabbed her hand and pulled her along. She shone her torch around the roots of another giant tree. That might offer some protection. Might. Was there anywhere else?

Suddenly it was upon them. The roar of the trees blowing as the wind ripped against branches and leaves. Rain bucketed down, stinging their eyes. A branch crashed behind them as the girls fled to the next tree like frightened animals, escaping. Then, like the door in Alice's Wonderland dream, a gaping hollow in a massive tree trunk before them became visible in their fading torch-light. It was dark and sinister, but they had no choice. "Quick, in here," said Jo and she pulled Andi in after her.

They huddled together in the dark, stiff with cold and dread. The bush that had been silent moments before now erupted in a tearing, blowing, shredding, shaking roar. Rain pelted trees; rivers of mud ran as Jo shone her torch periodically outside to see the forest floor gush past. Then, with an enormous and violent shudder, the walls of the inside of the tree where they were cowering, shook viciously as hail was thrown through the forest. Large rocks of ice piled high against the trees about them. The strong smell of eucalyptus swelled as trees were stripped of their leaves. Their light tracksuits over their thin summer T-shirts were soaking wet. When the wind whistled into the cavity in their tree-trunk, it was like someone opened a refrigerator door and blasted them with icy air.

They shivered in their dark den, crying with fatigue and anxiety, jumping as they heard another branch or tree crash to the ground nearby. They wrapped their arms around each other for comfort and warmth, and then, as there was no possible way they could sustain the tension any longer, they dozed in a fitful, exhausted sleep.

* * *

They were jolted awake by voices. "We're here! Help! We got lost! Hello?" They staggered out of their wooden cave into the crisp, clear morning-light of a world washed clean from the overnight storm. The forest was ravaged. Branches were fallen, torn from trunks bearing the gashing wounds from their traumatic survival of the vicious, freak gale. Underneath the cold chill, banks of melting hail lay piled in scattered lumps.

What they saw took their breath away. It never occurred to them that they would be safer lost. Two wild looking men, dressed in rags, long hairy beards touching the tops of their dirty overalls stood staring at them, stunning their

22

cursing into silence. They carried a tangle of traps and stuff over their shoulders. Jo and Andi held each other's hand for reassurance. They couldn't say anything. They stood stiff and frozen from their night in a tree. Fear strangled them.

Finally, one of the men broke into a slimy, broken toothed leer. "Whata do we have here then chaps?" He dug the other fellow in the ribs and sniggered.

Jo felt the hairs on the back of her neck rise. Andi pleaded silently with God. "God! Send the biggest, toughest sword-bearing angel and stand him smack bang in front of us. Please Jesus! Please!"

The other man looked curiously at them. He had an ugly, jagged scar that ran down the side of his face and across his eyelid. It turned his eye at a weird angle. He twisted his head strangely as if it assisted his vision. "Lost – you say?"

The girls nodded mutely.

"Where ya from?"

Andi swallowed hard. "The camp site…" she said hoarsely. "It's not far… it's just that we don't know which way… we got off the track."

The scarred, palsied eyed man turned his head so he could see them out of his good eye. "Ya bin out all night then? In the storm?"

The girls nodded. "We found this hollow tree."

The other brute leered again showing his rotted teeth, "That's our tree ya camped in. You made ya-self at home at our place… there'll be a price for ya boarding and lodgin' then…" and he staggered toward them.

The girls stepped back. The eye-fellow hauled him back in, holding him by his grimy, ragged jacket-collar. "Now you go being a gentleman, you filthy low-life. They're lost. And they dunno the camp is washed out. It might've been their folks…"

A look of realisation registered on the girls' faces. "Washed out? Was any one hurt?" asked Jo immediately, her head full of all the sounds and images of last night's storm flashed though her mind.

The toothless guy sniggered humourlessly. "Dunno if they's was hurt or not… but they's…" He flung the traps off his back and it followed with a string of possums that fell limp and hard onto the ground with a thud.

"Gone?" echoed Andi weakly, eyeing the dead things in front of her. "The camp site? The campers? Everyone?"

Jo gasped in horror at the sight. She froze. Normally she would have given them a piece of her mind about destroying protected wildlife in a National Park, but the look on the face of the creepy guy who'd thrown down the possums, silenced her. The other guy looked weirder, with his sightless eye and all, but this other fellow made her flesh crawl. He had 'dangerous' written all over him. Jo closed her mouth and said nothing. They looked at the soft furry creatures that last night they had watched in animated fascination, lying lifeless on the ground. They backed up against the tree, shaking all over. They started to cry.

The palsy-eyed man looked at them strangely. An expression rather like compassion registered on his face. "Ya could of been a bit gentla like – don't ya reckon?"

"They're all alone... standing there in their under-drawers. That's what I reckon."

Something snapped in the other man's face. His eye twitched in anger. "You filthy low-life scum! Strapper, you so much as *look* at a hair on their heads and I'll shoot you to kingdom-come. Ya wanta touch? You try... and I'll..." He delicately began to describe all sorts of unmentionable and dexterous things he could do with his long, antiquated rifle. His low voice was threatening. It seemed he meant every word *quite* literally.

"Well gee, Perce... when did you get all holy and righteous? No one knows they're here. No one'll miss em."

"You!" and he strung out a volley of cusses that left the other man reeling. Then he lifted the butt of his musket and clouted him across the chin. "Get out of here, you...." and he was gripped by a wordless rage.

He flung the creep across a log, and he sprawled head long in the wet forest floor. Strapper staggered to his feet and let out a barrage of uncouth adjectives. "Okay! Okay! But I want my pelts! They's mine! I want my cut!" He stood yelling abuse and threats through his dirty, half decayed teeth. "You filthy thieving convict! I'll have you reported! You'd be goin' to Norfolk!"

"Strapper, you're a low, belly scraping snake! I wouldn't put it past the likes of you. Here – take ya mangy pelts! You be leaving me two. Now, git ya mangy flea-bitten scalp outa my face. Or ya won't have one to show about." He flung a string of possums at his feet with one of the traps. "Git outa here!"

He gathered up his possums in a flurry, grabbed his traps and skedaddled away among the trees, like a hunted, abused old dog.

When he was gone, the man sat down on his haunches, breathing heavily, the scarred side of his face averted. He said nothing. Slowly the girls registered he was waiting... waiting for them. They wiped their pale, tear-streaked faces on their sleeves, their shoulders still heaving from sobs that they tried so hard to suppress. They focused on this ugly, grotesque man who had been their guardian. Had he been the angel they had prayed for in disguise?

"Well. Me name is Percival Holmes," he offered officially. He swallowed and looked away again. "Umm. Your clothes... where are ye clothes?"

"Well. This is it. Our other stuff is at the camp."

"Oh. Then I'll take ya back to the camp now if ya like. It ain't far."

* * *

3.

Jo shook herself. She felt like she was walking in a coma. She pulled Andi to her feet. "Come on. We'd better go and find out."

They dragged themselves along behind Percival Holmes as he skirted comfortably around fallen branches and large trees that had been markers on a decimated track. Nothing about this bizarre hermit made sense. It was clear he didn't meet many people. His manner was like his name – strange and official for someone who was a homeless guy. He didn't look back. He expected they would follow... and they did.

The ravages of the intense storm wiped anything that looked familiar away. Was this the same forest that they walked in so freely last night? It seemed like a dozen lifetimes had passed in the night and now they were walking out on the other side into an unknown world. They felt an urgency to get back to camp. The others would be worried – unless… What if that creep Strapper was right and they had been completely washed out?

Finally, Percival paused at the edge of a clearing. He seemed reluctant to proceed. Jo and Andi looked in horror at the trampled ground. Every blade of grass had been pulverised into a muddy pulp. Nothing remained. Trees were sawn off and straggled limbs were strung out around the trees. Muddy white canvas sheets hung limply over props in makeshift fly-tents and a few men stood talking by campfires dressed only in their trousers as the morning quickly became muggy as the sun became hot. Not a real tent in sight. Not a familiar person anywhere. It was all gone.

"Jo…" said Andi quietly. "I don't like this. Surely one storm would not have done this?"

Jo stared with disgust. "Who are these people? This is not a recovery crew. They have vandalised everything that was not damaged by the storm. It is obscene!" She surveyed the scene before her. Her rage mounting as she realised that there were dead animal skins pegged on trees, and no doubt, roasting on the fire.

"Go on Missies… They'll be pleased enough to know you're a-right."

"Mr Holmes?" Andi was tentative now. "I don't think this is our camp-ground. There are no toilets, or anything. This is a different one."

"Not your…." He looked at her quizzically. "Don't know of any other camps about. It's an isolated spot. Can't imagine where…"

"Could you come with us then? Maybe they'll know…" There was security in his coarse but sincere protection now.

"Ohhh, I'd rather not Missies. Got my pardon ticket. Don't really want to get tangled in this affair now. You just go on."

"Pardon-ticket?" Andi looked at him; her face went a shade paler. She clutched Jo's shoulder tightly, as she took another look at this cock-eyed possum-hunter. Trust them to fall into the hands of a convicted felon – or was he just a victim of mental illness? Andi remembered snippets of the angry accusations and threats that flew between the partners. She felt swamped in the horror of their predicament. Or perhaps "Pardon Ticket" was his eccentric way of explaining parole. She stepped back, afraid. "Have you escaped... from somewhere?"

"I've got my ticket. I'm a free man," he said defensively.

"*Were* you...a..." She retreated again.

"Convict. Aye, you can say it. Guess it's the truth."

"Convict?" That was not exactly how Andi was going to say it. Prisoner, detainee, inmate maybe... but not *convict*.

A resigned look passed over his face. Would he ever be able to say goodbye to the ghosts from the past that lurked around his shoulders? Once it meant he was constantly angry. Now it just wearied him. "Yeah," he sighed. He understood their fear.

Jo noticed some men pause their conversations and were looking around. She ducked down and pulled Andi away from the camp. "What did you do?" she demanded of Percy, without fully realising they could have a murderer as a guide.

"The usual. I got caught... poaching," he confessed.

"Poaching? Eggs?" Jo burst out laughing, and Andi quickly smothered the noise with her hand. "Now that's a crime that threatens public safety!"

"...on crown land," he continued matter-of-factly, but a smile materialized around the corner of his good eye.

Andi stared at him. Jo sobered and didn't even flinch as Andi's grip on her shoulder became tighter and tighter. "Those men... in the camp... what are they doing?" Andi asked.

"Standin' around."

"No – why are they here, doing what…?"

"Packing up my guess – getting ready to leave. The storm threw them. They'd be going back today no doubt."

"Leave what? Who are they?"

"Timber-getters. Timbers are a-wanting for the new buildings in the colony."

"Colony?" Jo and Andi said at the same time. Jo looked at him intensely.

"Yeah – the new Gov'nor's pushing major building projects. Some of 'em are quite flash."

"What year is this?" asked Andi presently.

"Don't know exactly. I cum in '98… had 2 years in the chain-gang, 5 years in service…been out for nine or ten, I reckon, maybe more."

Jo looked at him. He was really crackers. "A ripe one," her Grandad would've said. "That makes this year…ooooh about…" She stopped. "Unless…"

"Who is the Prime Minister?" asked Andi suddenly.

"Dunno."

"Well, you must know," Andi persisted.

"Why? Prime Minister of what… chain-gangs and public works?" It was his turn give a subdued sort of chuckle.

"Well – what did you call him? "Gov'nor" then… you know – top guy."

"Aye, that depends…"

"Depends on what?"

"Some still thinks Bligh's the man. He's gone but that don't stop 'em none… I reckon he's his own biggest supporter me-self."

"Bligh?" Andi was astounded: "as in 'Captain Bligh', as in the Rum Governor? Surely not!"

"This Gov'nor – he seems decent enough. He may be just..." Suddenly he stopped. "You ain't seem the types to be interested in politics."

"Neither are you." Andi stared. It could *not* be true! Not again. Did he mean *1798* when he came here? Her calculations meant this year, now – was in the vicinity of 1815. That is over *two centuries ago!* "This is so unfair. Why can't we go somewhere nice?" she exclaimed as she slumped on a log.

Jo shook her head and sat down on a rock. "Were you really sent here from England as a convict for... ?"

"Poaching." Percival stood leaning on a tree, infinitely patient, somewhat amused. His story was not that different from others he knew.

Andi knew this story too. She had read it in history books. She jumped up, wanting to show him she understood. "You were poaching rabbits to feed your starving family and they arrested you. Is that right?"

He smiled then – a crooked ironic grin. Could an ugly, ex-con like him get the sympathy of two strange displaced young girls? These girls... they would be younger than his baby sister would be now. He knew he would not win votes with the truth, but he was sick of living with the lies. "Not quite..."

Jo interrupted before Andi launched in with some other theories. "Let him tell us what happened."

"There was a group of us. We got caught hunting stag. One hung, the rest of us were transported."

"Your friend was *executed* for shooting a deer?"

He snorted at the very thought. "Ain't exactly a friend... more like business partner."

"You call stealing – a business!"

"Well, a good size stag brought good money. Not much else did. One or two would set you up real good. But..." His voice trailed off.

"But... you couldn't stop at two?"

"Well, I weren't the only one. It was two for the others as well. We managed quite a lot, in the end, before..."

"Surely you knew you'd get caught?" It seemed a foolhardy approach to financial planning, doomed to failure from the outset.

"I was gunna get married." He lips warped in a cynical twist; his crooked, sightless eye clouded in distant memories.

"To who? What was her name?"

"Annie."

"So, you didn't poach the stag because you were starving?" Andi was disappointed. Starvation at least made such choices understandable... even justified.

"Na." He smiled at them again. And then added, "Poachin' rabbits kept *that* thief from the door."

* * *

What now? Andi didn't want to go into that camp full of strangers. And she didn't want to go with this eccentric ex-con turned hermit. *God – I don't know what to do! What are we going to do?*

It was as if Percival understood their dilemma. "This really ain't your camp – aye?"

The girls' nodded apologetically.

"Hmmm." He stood there, wondering how circumstances always managed to extract a sympathy vote from him. Isn't that how he got stuck in this barbaric place in the first place? Listening to another's plight when his own circumstances were enough for one man to carry. He should've taken his cut and left the others with their fingers in the pie. But that was not how he was made. If they helped him, it was the decent thing to help them in return. Yet they didn't help him – not when they were caught red-handed. They just traded names for whatever elusive promises they offered. And those promises never eventuated anyway.

Percy knew what it was like to feel as lost as these girls. But he learnt to read the bush like one of those gentlemen books. Some Aborigines befriended him. They saved his life and taught him how to eat and drink and live like a King in this most barren, God-forsaken land on the planet. Gradually he looked at it differently. He saw beauty in the rugged landscape, where once he only yearned for the wide sweeping fenlands of Lincolnshire. Now he saw majesty instead of adversity; emancipation where he experienced the exile of slavery.

He peered at the girls through his seeing eye. "I know a place where ya can stay until we find ya folks. Mrs Gartery will take ya in. She'll give ya proper clothes to wear." He recognised their look of timid scepticism. "I keep her in fresh meat. She owes me some dues," he explained.

* * *

Mrs Gartery stood and looked at the girls. She blinked her thick red eyelashes thoughtfully. "I dunno Percy. How they could be lost, like you say? More likes they's in trouble and be running away." She didn't address Andi or Jo. She talked as if they were not even in the room. She didn't pause. "Girls running around in the scrub in their underwear has got to be trouble. And I've got enough trouble without inviting it in. I'm reckoning you be tryin' somewhere else." She stared at Andi. "And that one. She must have some sort of disease, that caused her hair to go like that."

Jo rolled her eyes. "It's dyed. Not contagious."

Mrs Gartery turned her back and spoke firmly to Percy. "Go. And take them with you."

Percy stood unmoved. "Aye, but you've got room?"

"I do. But like I said, I'll not be givin' it to 'em!"

Percy gathered up the skinned possums that were lying on the table in a cleanly laundered, but stained sheet. Revolting flies buzzed around it. "Guess we be goin' then."

"Well, ya can't take my food. We be needin' that for supper."

"Ain't your food 'til ya eat it. Ya can't eat it till ya pay for it."

"But I explained, Percy. I can't pay until..."

"Well... that can't be helped."

"But I've been good for it in the past! You know I'll pay."

He grunted and walked towards the door.

"Alright. Alright! You crazy, goony-eyed tyrant!"

"So, we're clear, they be staying until I can locate their folks."

"But you said that you had no way of knowing where to start. They could be here until the good Lord returns! They can't stay indefinitely!"

"Now Mrs Gartery, you've got more than most around here. You eat meat every night. You got naught to complain about."

"Ahem… excuse me, but we are…" inserted Andi, trying to be polite.

Mrs Gartery's eyebrows shot up high as if she had forgotten they were even there. "Humph!" She turned on her heel and left the room.

The house was a small and primitive 'wattle-and-daub' hut. The walls were plastered with mud and it smelt constantly damp as if the moisture could not escape. There were only four small rooms and one of those was set up like a miniature dormitory with tiered bunks and rough bare blankets.

Percy shrugged as she left the room. "I ain't seen her this testy in a long time. I reckon that sailor must be due back soon. Comes in with the fleets and then goes again. You'll be seein' him soon enough. He won't give much trouble once he gets drunk. I'll be back in two or three days – to top up the larder. I'll pass on any news then."

He disappeared out the door into the surrounding scrub, leaving the girls abandoned on a desert island. They waited for a while, but Mrs Gartery did not come back, so they went into the bunkroom. In a makeshift sort of way, the rough timbered beds had the look of nautical berths. They were short and narrow and spartan. Only two beds were obviously occupied. It was impossible to sit on them, so the girls sat on the floor and pulled their knees up around their ears.

"I want to go home so badly," whispered Andi in a small voice. She looked at her friend sitting beside her. Jo said nothing either. She wanted to be brave but had lost her bravado. Andi tried to remember other times when they had helped people in strange places. But she couldn't. All she could see was the stark uncomfortable room and a grumpy woman who didn't want them. Could any real dreams be planted in such barren place? Andi didn't think so. And it never occurred to her just yet, that her 'other life' was living proof it could be so.

* * *

Presently Mrs Gartery called them into the sitting room. *Sitting room* was a rather generous term. They stood. Jo tried to guess Mrs Gartery's age, but she gave up. Her face looked oldish… well, worn maybe, but she had only a touch of grey in amongst the rich red hair that was pulled back in a bun. She certainly wasn't pretty, but she had a sort of presence that made you remember you were in *her* house.

"Every girl that comes here gets this same talk. I have rules, and while you abide the rules, you can stay. I gave me word to Percy on that. But this is not a house of ill-repute and I ain't going to abide nonsense." Without any elaboration she laid down the law. The girls knew very well these points were not negotiable.

Finally, she paused. "Now is everything understood?" They nodded mutely. "One last thing. The good book says,

'He who doth not work, doth not eat'. I stand by that very simply. If you don't do your chores, you miss dinner. There's scant enough to go around some nights as it is. The girls leave when I find them a satisfactory position. That is the *only* thing that is different for you two, like Percival said. But you are not to tell any of the others. It will be just the same for you, as for them... right up to the minute you go. Until then, you will work as I say. If we do our work, God will provide. That's all."

She barely paused, but Andi timidly raised her hand. Mrs Gartery's eyebrows arched up, this time in surprise. "Hmmm?"

"Well, it's not really a question... more like a comment. I noticed that you quote the Bible. I wanted you to know that we try to do what God would want and I think that is why we are here. We'll be no trouble at all... really."

Andi was not sure what response she expected from this confession, but it wasn't the curt, "Pfft! Well, we'll see about that!" which was tossed at them as she dumped a change of clothes in the bunkroom. She ordered them to get dressed and start their chores. She paused at the door and looked severely at Andi. "I don't know what's going on with your hair, but you will cover it up and wear that bonnet whenever you are outside this room. Understood?"

She timidly nodded as she left. Jo grimaced soberly as they clambered into the long, patched, and drab colonial skirts they were given. "I think we just landed in a work-house. So much for Christian Charity."

That night Jo and Andi were given cooking lessons in the semi-detached, outside kitchen. They had possum stew. No vegetables. A small hard loaf of bread, more like a rock, was rationed into six portions. There was a long trestle table out the back, which was where they served the meal. As the plain and chipped plates were set down, Mrs Gartery stood at the head of the table. Suddenly three other people materialised out of nowhere and they reached out and held hands in a ring around their table. On some unknown cue, they all said, "We thank Thee Lord for Thy daily mercies and the provision of this food, Amen."

Mrs Gartery remained standing and looked over at Jo and Andi who had sat down on the form-bench exhausted. She waited wordlessly until Andi dug Jo in the side and they stood back to their feet. "Miriam and Bridget, please allow me to introduce Joanne-ah and Andrea." Miriam was older, and Bridget probably was about their age. Miriam had plain features, a big-boned frame and limp, flat hair. Bridget on the other hand had light curly hair that bobbed in an unruly tangle around her pert little face. It gave her an interesting look.

Turning to Jo and Andi she said, "Miriam and Bridget came here about four months ago. We are in the process of locating a suitable position for 'em." She sat down. They all followed suit.

There was another girl with thick strawberry blond hair and large eyes, who appeared to be about seven or eight years old. She was completely ignored. They all sat and started eating. Jo leaned over to the girl and whispered, "Hi, I'm Jo.... What's your name?"

The girl looked into her stew with great concentration. She pushed at it with her spoon and started to eat. Jo figured the girl didn't hear and tapped her on the sleeve. "Hi, I'm…"

"Joanna! Would you be polite enough to allow Jane to eat her meal in peace?"

Jo sat up straight and started pushing her stew around her plate. Okay… apparently chatting was considered the height of ill manners. Her Mum had always been tired from working shifts and was not big on dinner being a social event. Jo agreed. Eating together was seriously overrated.

Andi tried to eat. She just kept seeing the mother possum and two little babies clinging to her back. The whole thing repulsed her.

Suddenly Mrs Gartery stood up. "We return our thanks to You our Lord for this food. Bless our night with Your protection. Amen." The others murmured 'Amen' in unison; their plates already cleaned and mopped up with their brittle bread. The other girls whipped the plates away, scraped their leftover stew back into the cast-iron cooker and quickly washed up in a small amount of cold water.

Andi looked on in horror. Didn't they know that that sticking half eaten food back in the pot could give them food poisoning? She stacked away the plates and tried not to gag. They didn't use hot water or have refrigerators, yet they all looked healthy enough. What would they ever do if they got sick here?

Jo looked at the others going about their chores with dutiful efficiency. She picked up a brush-broom and began to sweep the compacted dirt floor. Was everything about duty and work? She felt it draining the energy from her.

Andi grabbed Jo's hand as the others went to retire. "Come out here, we desperately need to chat." They sat on a log a short way from the house looking into the scrub, the dim light from the dirty broken lamp cast long shadows out the shuttered window. Andi was taking deep breaths. "This place is so primitive!"

"You're telling me! I feel like I'm being drugged into some sort of zombie state. Everyone is so morbid. I almost wish Percy would come back. Least he knew how to smile — even if it was a bit crooked."

"We need to pray…"

"Girls! Here! Now! Straight away!" Mrs Gartery tall frame loomed over them as she hissed in the dark, harsh and grating.

They jumped. They'd done their jobs. Couldn't they have just a second together? Andi stood up quickly. "Oh, I hate this place!" she muttered.

Mrs Gartery pulled them inside and slammed the door. "Don't *ever* do that again!"

"Do what?" asked Andi.

"You insolent child! You know very well!"

"Pretty sure we don't," Jo said sassily.

Even Andi was getting jack of all the accusations. "We have done all our chores. We just wanted to talk…"

"Don't back-chat me, you snotty nosed little upstarts. I don't know where you think you've come from or how long you're going to be here, but I'll not be accused of neglecting my charges. Not you and not anyone!"

Andi's eyes opened wide in shock. "No one's accusing you of neglect." Well... not much.

"And what happens when some native runs you through with a spear? Sitting out there like ducks with a sign! Foolishness! Not all of 'em are sympathetic to Percy's association here. You absolutely thoughtless fools! Your upper-class lot are not going to stand by then and say I'm innocent! It'll be my fault for sure... and then my neck!" Her pupils were wide with anger. "I've established a life here with my daughter. Don't you dare jeopardise that with your careless, inconsiderate, privileged ways!" They stood stunned as she stormed into the next room. Jo and Andi had no idea what she really meant, except it was a warning. That part of the message had been quite distinct.

* * *

True to his word Percival came back three days later. The girls felt bad he was searching for a campsite that wouldn't exist for another two hundred years, and yet somehow, they didn't want him to give up looking and disappear out of their lives. He had saved them from the hands of that brute, Strapper. Perhaps he was their connection to the future.

As he looked at them, his deformed eye ogling at them from a peculiar angle, it was difficult not to feel revolted. Immediately Andi felt her conscience prick. On one hand she wanted him to stick around. On the other, it seemed she could barely look at him because of his shabby appearance. Even the smell was dreadful, and ... that eye! It was hideous. She swallowed and turned away. She tried to stay on his undamaged side. It wasn't so bad if she didn't have to look at his eye.

Percy was not oblivious to their reaction to his appearance. Yet that was not important just now. They were young…and unseasoned. He guessed they had been raised in one of those posh-English glasshouses. They seemed so fresh and tender, completely disconnected from the weather of the world outside the greenhouse. He couldn't understand his sympathy for them. He felt only contempt for every other Sterling he knew. But these girls? And he only had bad news for them. For some reason he couldn't delight in the telling of it. He had news for Mrs Gartery as well.

The girls were scratching in the rock-hard ground that was barely an excuse for a vegetable garden. It seemed so hopeless trying to coax any life out of the baked land. Cultivation of fresh food was not successful here. The garden was just behind the house and they could hear Percy talking inside. If they didn't have to look at him, he sounded pretty normal. "Now Polly Gartery, I know it's true. They've seen 'em down the coast some. It's on its way."

Her voice was cross. "They aren't expected back for months yet. It won't be him."

"Aye maybe. But I thought ya should know." She said nothing, yet her silence was eloquent. Percy continued. "I got a wallaby for ya. Once you dry it, you'll be set for a while. I can come back when you're out."

"Percival Holmes you're makin' yourself scarce on account of him!"

"Polly Gartery – the man's your husband. He won't be expectin' the likes of me to be supplyin' you with food."

"I have to get it from somewhere."

"Not sure he'll see it like that."

"We would've starved long ago if it weren't for you. Nothin' untoward goes on." Polly paused; her voice resigned. "How many days then?"

"A bit more than a week. That's all."

There was a ponderous silence. Polly started to walk up and down... rubbing the side of her head thoughtfully. Her anxiety showed in the steps she took around the room. It was motion, and somehow it helped her think things through. "The girls will have to camp out; the first night at least. Can ya stick around for 'em?"

Percy nodded, as Polly walked around the room. He followed her with his good eye as she continued processing out loud. "They'll be safe enough if they's with you. I would send Janie away too if I thought I couldn't bluff me way through."

"I'll be goin' now. Hang out the scarf like ya do. I'll meet 'em on dusk at the tree. I's got a stash of rum that'll quiet him down some. It'll be in the usual place."

"I thank ya. Couldn't afford the way he sloshes through it. It's the devil's own potion and yet I give it to him. I don't know how the good Lord'll forgive me for it; and yet I don't know how I'd do without it."

"Never thought I'd hear the day when you'd admit you're beat."

"I just know how it is. It's been too long to hope it could be different."

"I'm sorry to hear it, Polly Gartery. You're a good woman."

"Well, you're alone in that opinion. But granted, I like it that you have one."

The girls went back to scratching in the soil. He saluted briefly as he went passed. "She'll be on edge till the fleet gets goin' again. Take care of her, girls."

Andi and Jo looked at each other. Take care of the work-house overseer? No one needed to look after her. She was quite capable all by herself.

* * *

4.

Percy had been right about one thing. Mrs Gartery was edgy. She was tetchy about anything that was not done exactly how she expected it. That covered just about everything since nothing *could* be done well in these appalling conditions. Eight-year-old Jane retreated even further into her quiet, timid little shell. She reminded Jo of the little pig-nosed turtles she saw at an aquarium once. They pulled their heads in as quick as anything when she tapped on the glass.

Mrs Gartery took the girls with her on her trips to the wharf. It was the hub of the colony, around where commerce and the workings of the settlement revolved. Very much like a village market. Small work-gangs of convicts moved under the watchful eye of red-coated soldiers. The sight of their tall black hats and long pointed bayonets sent shivers up Mrs Gartery's spine, and she instinctively turned away until they had passed. Even so, every day she would be down at the wharf asking about news of what was happening in the colony. With a new urgency, Mrs Gartery looked for suitable positions for Miriam and Bridget. They had a week to find something before the next fleet of convicts arrived saturating an already diminished work market for women.

Polly Gartery knew these girls needed someone who could advocate for them with influence. She did what she could, but she was not the right person. No one would listen to her. She had on her back the scars of a cat-of-nine. She prayed daily that God would send someone who could make a difference. Still, she tried. Polly approached men and proprietors, ladies and soldiers. Without exception they looked down their nose, and gave some sleazy, inappropriate offer for her girls. It seemed that finding a decent position was nigh impossible, but still she persisted. If Jane were one of those standing on the wharf of some foreign exotic land, alone and helpless, she would appreciate someone trying to genuinely help her.

Her mother's heart throbbed for these girls. She didn't feel the same about the two girls that Percy had brought to her though. Why he would even bother with them, she didn't know. Deep down she knew they didn't need her help. They were *Sterling*: gentry, or from one of the militia families. That was obvious, by their tight and "proper" grammar; their religious clichés; their disregard for common colony rules, and their revulsion of ordinary food that sustained them when others had died. No, they didn't need her help, and the sooner they went back to their set, the better.

She paced the timbered wharf, her long, frayed petticoat snagging on the rough splintered beams. A drunken fisherman reeled over to them and Mrs Gartery manoeuvred her girls away from him. A gentleman strode across the road helping the lady on his arm, steering clear of mud that the constant foot traffic would not let dry. "Wait here girls," Polly said quietly as she approached the couple boldly.

"Good morning, Sir. I am Mrs Gartery. I have two girls in my charge, and I'm looking to place them in a position. Would your good wife be needing house help? An attendant – perhaps? Both girls are polite, comely and attend their Christian duties."

The man brushed her off. She was obviously poverty stricken. It was not appropriate to talk with her. Not in public. But Polly would not be put off. This happened every time. She never got used to it, yet she pushed through their prejudice because the girls needed her to. She turned to the lady. "Madam, such help would be fitting for a lady such as yourself. You know good help is not easy to come by. These girls are not convicts. If you wait for the fleet, you will only have felons to choose from." Inside Polly winced. This was her life she was talking disdainfully about.

The slight lady paused and considered Polly. She moved her parasol out of the way and looked at Polly's basic attire in distaste. "George, the woman has a point. I don't know if I want to wait for the fleet. We don't know when it'll be arriving. It could be months away."

George obviously had no interest in the situation. "Honestly Eliza, must we consider this now? There is plenty of time..."

Eliza Thornton glanced over at the girls standing a way off. "The one with bonnet and dark hair might be suitable." She indicated Andi with a very condescending point of her gloved finger.

"Sorry madam, only two are available to take positions: Miriam – the one in the brown skirt, and Bridget, there with the curly hair."

Mrs Thornton sighed dramatically. She was *so* inconvenienced. "Bring them here then."

The girls shuffled over, and they stood behind Mrs Gartery submissively. A position like this would be much better than having to marry an impoverished farmer. A wife offered free labour and the necessary marriage certificate required to draw supplies of seed from the Governor's store.

"George, I can't see why we don't just take these and be done with it. It would save a great deal of discomfort on my part by having to wait." Eliza sighed most wearily and patted her forehead, as beads of perspiration clustered on her brow. She pointed to Miriam. "Can you cook?"

"Yes Ma'am, and I do housekeeping." She didn't elaborate that Percy's wallaby stew was her speciality. The other's loved it when Miriam cooked dinner.

"Well, if they had decent clothes, I think they might be presentable. She looked at Polly, and nodded: a short, abrupt, no-fuss nod. "I'll take them both."

"Both?" Polly reiterated.

"Is there a problem? Don't the girls get along?"

"No. No, not at all. This is very good news! Thank you, Ma'am. I trust that their service will be a great source of comfort and industry to you both." She paused, and then quickly continued before the moment was lost. "Ma'am, if you be knowing of any others needing good help... girls are coming to me all the time."

The lady was indifferent. She was momentarily satisfied and that was all that mattered. Bridget and Miriam gathered their bags, gave a quick round of hugs and they were walking back around the mud, across the street into their new life. Just like that.

* * *

The rest of the week went quickly. The news that the fleet was coming was only derived from Percy's Aboriginal contacts. There was no official notification of its arrival. How could there be? The sight of the large billowing sails as they tipped around the harbour's head was the only herald the colony ever received of their next contact with the English Motherland. So, when Polly saw the large white cloud of sail as the fleet entered the harbour, she was none too surprised. Percy's information was not always reliable, but it could never be totally disregarded.

Polly left the wharf then. She knew exactly how much time she had to prepare. She took the girls back to the hut and quickly obliterated any sign they had been there. They stuffed their things in a coarse cloth bag and Polly ushered them out into the bush. They stopped by a large coachwood tree. Its thick, straight trunk was mottled with moss and lichens as it stretched up into the forest canopy. Polly told them to wait here for Percy. There were basic signs of an old campsite, and an old bark shelter, nestled back in low growing trees. Andi shivered involuntarily. "What about the Aborigines? You said they could attack."

"Just at the moment, angry natives are the least of your problems. You stay put. You've got a loaf of bread, some flour and lard in this bag. Ration it with Percy and he'll look after ya until it's okay to come back. I gotta go. Janie is at home by herself."

She left quickly, palpitations thumping the inside of her chest. "God – protect my girl, my little Janie… and these two. And me… if…" Polly paused. Asking protection for herself seemed a mighty selfish petition. It was almost that she believed that she didn't deserve safety, that somehow her life was an ongoing punishment for past sins. She hated the fact she wasn't stronger… she hated who she became when he was around.

The girls saw the fear in her eyes… and they could not comprehend how one person could inspire such dread and trepidation. A capable advocate had turned into faint-hearted mush before their eyes. What threat could be great enough to warrant this Hansel and Gretel journey into the bush? "I feel like we've been dumped like a couple of stray cats. It's kinda scary out here," she said looking around.

"Yeah well, I'm glad we don't have to go back there. You saw her. She's scared."

Andi looked sincerely into Jo's face, and she had to admit her own fears seemed petty in comparison. "I guess you're right," she conceded.

Jo grunted. She didn't want to be right all the time – especially about this. "Why are we put in situations where there is nothing we can do? Wouldn't it be better if we landed in the governor's house or something… where we could do something that would make a difference?"

Andi looked at the low shrubs and watched a bowerbird jump and bounce, gathering common little treasures to decorate his bower, making it unique and beautiful. He added some green berries to his emerald-green collection. Andi was floundering. Her faith was taking a battering. "What I don't get is how Mrs Gartery says she honours God, which she probably does in her way... but how is it helping her? This is a terrible mess!"

Jo closed her eyes and saw the timid set to Mrs Gartery's jaw as she hurried back towards her house. She knew the answer to this question. "It doesn't seem to be helping her at all." Was it wrong to admit that out loud?

"...*and* she resents the fact we are here adding to her problems. Don't deny it Jo. You know she does!" Andi added, feeling powerless and angry.

"Well, I don't get it." Jo shrugged. "But I've been thinking about wanting good things for others. Perhaps... even though it is just about survival, at the moment, perhaps we can hold a dream for the future despite of what it looks like now."

Andi looked at her friend. Would Jo finally start to trust God... in a place like this? But honestly, this felt too hard – even for God. She was grateful she could talk to Jesus about what was bugging her; knowing that he wouldn't judge or condemn her doubts. Keeping the communication lines open, her Mum said, that was her responsibility.

Andi looked for a spot of blue through the top of the trees and focused on that. It was horrible watching someone so boldly advocating for others one moment, and then suddenly become so frightened the next. There was probably good reason for it though. And then there was Percy. She didn't understand any of it. Wisps of cloud floated across her patch of blue and she whispered a prayer in her heart. "I don't get it, but I'm glad you're here with us."

The warmth of the mid-morning sun caressed the girls into a dozy sort of state. They thought about having a snack of plain bread, but decided it was too early yet. They might wait until later, closer to when Percy was to join them. That's if he was coming. They made themselves comfortable. They didn't want to think about what they would do if he didn't come before dark. What if their messages didn't connect?

Normally the girls always had something to talk about, but here it seemed harder. They didn't dare move. They had been lost before. Birds called and answered lazily. Jo tried to spot them in their perfectly camouflaged cover of green; the only evidence of their existence was the persistent calls that rang out over their heads. Andi passed their tall flask of water to Jo for a drink. They lay down and closed their eyes and waited.

* * *

By dusk the girls were restless as soft scattered clouds formed bundles of pink fairy-floss across the horizon. They were playing "I spy" and "Celebrity Head" without much enthusiasm. Jo was resigning for the third time. "I give in," she said rather fed up. "Can't you think of less obscure characters?"

"Where's the challenge in that?" said Andi. "I spy with my…" Suddenly Andi pointed overhead to the graceful shape of an eagle soaring on eddies of air currents. They held their breath as it glided low; it's dark brown feathers on its wide wings shining bronze in the sunlight. Its powerful dignity and silent majesty just drifted on air above them. Then higher and higher it circled up until it was merely a pinprick against the blue sky. Then it disappeared behind the tall shapes of the trees.

The atmosphere in their little camp by the coachwood tree changed. In a moment, the feeling of being discarded was transformed by the amazing grace and beauty they had witnessed. Andi was reminded again that God's hand was not far away. Just then, Percy materialised out of the scrub. He was sitting on his haunches, waiting silently. "Percy! We didn't think you would ever get here!"

"The Eagle… they are spiritual eyes to my mob. They told me you were here…"

"You? But you're not Aboriginal. You can't say that."

"Can if they adopt me. They're my family."

"How long were you there?"

He moved over to the old campfire. "Not long," he lied. He had watched three rounds of their games and was quite intrigued. These innocent games were a stark contrast to his late-night tavern pastimes back in the ol' country. Was it so long ago? It seemed like a million years. "We best make a fire. Grab some wood and we'd be startin' it."

"You've got matches?" asked Andi surprised.

He smiled. He certainly had no flint or tinder box. He never really thought about it now. He had a whole new way of looking at things. "I'll show you." The girls gathered small twigs, leaves and some larger sticks and branches. He produced two long thin sticks. One had a small regular charred depression in the end and he put the other thin, straight stick into it. Deftly he rolled it between his palms, up and down the length of the stick. Within moments, wisps of smoke appeared at the base. He blew and fanned the grass and leaves until a small yellow flame was coaxed into being. With a few more strategically placed twigs, a fire was made.

Jo was awed. "Can you teach me to do that? That is amazing!"

He shook his head. "Fire belongs to the men." He hoped that explained it enough, but he didn't really expect them to understand.

Jo opened her mouth to object, but something else caught her eye, and instead of the pert rejoinder that sat on her tongue, her mouth stayed open... wide like a suckerfish stuck to the side of a glass bowl. "We've got visitors..." she whispered.

In the recesses of the scrub an Aboriginal woman quietly stood, unashamed by her nakedness. Scars twisted across her breasts and dark arms forming wide patterns. She was holding a boat shaped container made of scooped out wood. She said nothing.

Percy stayed squatting by his fire. He didn't look at her but gently said something. Foreign words rolled off his tongue in muted tones. Andi listened to him enthralled. His voice was rich and gentle, almost... handsome. She couldn't believe it. Was this the same Percy that rescued them after the storm? The woman came forward cautiously. She squatted beside him, the swelling of her abdomen showed she was obviously expecting a baby. Percy looked at the girls. "This is Burilda, my gin... my wife."

"You're married?" said Jo shocked. She supposed him to be an authentic recluse.

"Burilda," repeated Andi. It sounded so soft. "What a beautiful name!"

"Aye. It means 'black swan'. She is my swan."

Once Jo would have gagged over something that sentimental, but as she watched the woman beside Percy, her graceful athletic body that was full with the promise of motherhood, and her shy, quiet smile, Jo had to admit, it was kind of romantic. The pride and affection Percy felt for Burilda was obvious.

Andi thought it the most perfect partnership in the world. One bore a disfiguring scar down the side of his face, and the other, so beautiful, was from a misunderstood and mysterious culture. That made it more charming to Andi. They were happy and relaxed together and that was the most enchanting of all.

* * *

Polly looked tentatively across the darkened room at her husband, his rough sailor hands clutching a stone bottle of rum. New colony regulations meant rum was no longer allowed to be used as currency. Sovereigns of the mother country was legal tender. But rum was still a highly prized commodity. It was hard to come by. He tried to find out how Polly acquired so much 'liquid gold'. He knew she couldn't be trusted. His unshaven face bristled as he sullenly eyed Polly with distaste. Once a convict – always a convict.

She said nothing, but hesitantly touched the broken, red and swollen welts, as her hair fell across on her cheek causing them to sting. He slouched in his low-slung chair and swigged large gulps of dark rum. James Gartery closed his eyes to the reality of this little hovel, that was supposed to be his castle. It was more than he could bear.

Jane crept in and whispered something to Polly. She looked pleading at her mother through a tear stained and bruised black eye, but her mother's only response was a tight-lipped desperate shake of her head. Even at eight years old, wise from being dragged from her childhood, she didn't always know when to stop. Janie, increasingly confident from the surly silence that settled over her father, persisted.

"Silence!" he bellowed, erupting in a rage like a disturbed bear in a cave. "Quiet! You have no respect!" He flung the mug in his hand and she squealed as it caught Janie across her brow.

"She didn't mean it James…honestly..." Polly turned to her daughter and whispered. "Quick – go to the tree. Now! Jane! You *must* go!"

"But Mama…"

"Now Janie, just go…"

"But Mama, what about you?"

"Janie… please!" and there were tears of desperation in her eyes. Jane picked up her skirts and ran out into the dim light of the settling dusk. She knew the tree her mother had arranged for the other girls to meet Percy. She flew to it, like a bird escaping from a snare, as she left behind the sounds of shattering furniture, drunken accusations, and muffled cries.

* * *

Jane stood by the fire clutching a thin shawl about her, trying to warm her skinny arms. Her body was shaking from the exertion of her flight. Percy's mouth was firm as he deftly skinned a possum and proceeded to peg it out. Burilda sat quietly by the fire, mashing some leaves and berries into a pulp, then checked some bark she was soaking in water. Finally, Percy stood. "Let's have a look at ya eye Miss Jane. Ya mother would want us to tend it."

"I'm fine." Jane stood resolutely tall. Her mother was brave; she could be too.

"Aye, I know Miss. But ya mother would feel better knowing we are tryin' to help."

"She doesn't know," Jane said defensively.

"Aye." Percy didn't know how far to push it. The girl was stubborn and proud – like her mother. But the eye seemed to be swelling tightly closed, and the skin was broken. On a kid so young it needed attention. He was particularly sensitive about eyes.

Andi stood up and came over to coax some co-operation. Poor Jane. "Percy's right. Your Mum would appreciate it."

"How would you know? You don't even know her!"

"I know she loves you. She would want you to be looked after."

Jane squeezed her eyes closed with a shudder. She had caused her Mum to cry. Her Mum never cried. She remembered the pained tears as she begged Jane to go. It was right she should suffer. Her pain was nothing when compared to her Mum's.

Jo came and pulled Andi back into the shadows. "Leave her alone. She's had enough for now."

"But her eye…"

"So what? It's just a black eye." Jo had watched with her heart in her mouth. For the first time since she could remember, Jo felt secretly relieved that she didn't even know her father. He never hit her like that because he had never been there. She used to be so jealous of real families with fathers at home. But she realised now that a family without love was not a 'real' family at all. It was better he had never been there.

Jane heard the words Jo had said in her defence and it comforted her. Yet Jane knew in her heart, she shouldn't even be here – not if she was brave. She should be at home, protecting her mother. Her eye was a trophy to that end. *Perhaps*, she thought, *if her father hit her – he'd hit her mother less.*

Jane knew her mum trusted Percy, but she wasn't so sure about Burilda. She heard people talk. But if her mum trusted Percy, and Percy trusted Burilda, perhaps she was okay. Still, she didn't want to die of poisoning. She'd heard stories about that too. She stared at the concoction that Burilda had prepared. If she put that on her eye, it would probably make it pop out. Her swollen lid was throbbing more. Jane sat down quietly and leant her forehead on her knees. Her long strawberry blond hair fell over her face as she tried to disguise the tears that fell in her lap. No one said anything for a very long time.

They wordlessly ate the roast meat that Percy had prepared. Burilda offered them some berries, but they tasted sour. Eventually, out of shear exhaustion, they lay down and slept.

* * *

James glared suspiciously at Polly as she cowered against the wall. He knew she was trying to get him drunk, but unlike the other times when he came ashore, he drank just short of the amount that would topple him over into a stupor. He was sure she was hiding something! His anger rose inside him. He would beat it out of her. She will tell him everything. A convict did not fool him! And the twerp of a girl – he could barely confess she was his daughter. More scandal: he spawned a "currency-lass", the term coined for colony-born girls. The disgrace of it all; he would never have any credibility as an Englishman while he had a convict wife and a currency-kid.

In the glazed state of booze-induced self-reflection, he saw his life as a string of disappointments, stolen ambitions, and piece-meal failures. Polly was the reason behind it all. It was all her fault. Without her, his life would not have turned out like this. He deserved vindication for the dud-bets he had placed at the roulette table of life.

* * *

The girls stirred in the early morning light of the forest. Mottled streaks of sunlight filtered through the glossy dew drenched leaves. Andi opened her eyes, briefly disorientated in that half-aware, half-asleep moment of waking. Wallabies nibbled grass contentedly in the small clearing and hopped away unperturbed for the greener pick of a nearby tuff of grass. Colourful crimson and blue rosellas chatted noisily as they nibbled gumnut flowers with acrobat confidence, swinging upside down, loudly egging each other on to wilder, more daring feats. Andi smiled at their audacious play and lay there quietly not wanting to disturb the delicate balance that teetered around her in the bush. For some reason the resilient Australian scrubland seemed fragile this morning. Jo stirred beside her.

Andi looked over to the fire. Something was roasting on a bushman's rotisserie above live coals… and even to her modern, sensitive nose it smelt very good.

Jo poked her in the back. "Look at that…" said Jo quietly.

Andi tried to ignore her. This could well be her purest back-to-nature experience yet… and wanted to protect this 'nature' moment an instant longer. Besides, she *had* been looking – at every delightful creature, every leaf and flower, every shade of green in the morning light. How extraordinary and miraculous nature is when you are right in the middle of it – so that you almost blend and become part of it.

But Jo was not interested in watching pouched joeys slip in and out of their mother's apron-pockets this morning. She jabbed Andi softly again. "Look at Percy…"

Andi sighed and rolled over. She gasped and held her breath. Percy was stripped to the waist, crouching over a dry pelt. He was rubbing down the skin with a rough rock, breaking the stiffness with long firm strokes. The light filtered down onto his body. Raised blue and red scars criss-crossed his back until the lines joined and merged into an ugly mangled mass of scar-tissue. Her stomach reeled as she listened to the old English pub ditty he was singing. The words cleverly interwove the trauma of his transportation into a musical tale of caution for the young and reckless.

Percy stood up and turned to the fire. The girls stared again. His chest also bore scares. Not the angry mass on his back, but bold patterned slashes across his chest of an aboriginal warrior. He continued to hum his song as he finished his pelts. Finally, he grabbed his shirt to put on and then he went to the fire to ready breakfast.

He looked up and saw the girls watching him. He smiled a crooked smile, full of mystery and intrigue. "Got some food here. Eat up. We're going somewhere today."

Even Jane stirred with interest. Distraction is what they needed, even craved. Percy pulled a damper made from their ration of flour out of the coals, wrapped in damp bark and leaves. It had a seasoned, smoked flavour that was the perfect accompaniment to their roast. Even Andi didn't want to ask exactly what they were eating. It was the first meal she had enjoyed since coming here.

* * *

James stood over Polly with a heavy hand. "Speak up! The truth!"

"I have told you. A trader comes – that is all."

He swore at her. "Fool! Ye think I am so dumb?"

"It is the truth. Upon my honour!"

"Honour?" He sneered a drunken hysterical laugh through his teeth. "Ye have *no* honour! Ye betray me! You, you..." He reeled off balance as he grabbed at her. His rough, salt weathered sailor's hand caught in her hair as she tried to duck out of the way. Her head jerked back.

Then with the abandoned reasoning of a coward, under the influence of the intoxicating opiate of lording it over the powerless, he grabbed a leather collar hanging by the door.

Polly stared in horror as he tightened his grip on another fistful of bronzed hair. "James! What are you doing?" He clamped it around her neck, roughly bruising her soft flesh.

"Ye're going back to where you belong. I don't have to put up with this!"

"Whatever do you mean? How can you say that? I have looked after Jane so well! James! Don't!"

He narrowed his eyes dangerously. "She's not here, is she? Ye've stolen her."

"Stolen Jane? You are mad. I was afraid…"

"Afraid? Ye know nothing yet! Where is she?" And he grabbed a rope.

"At a friend's place…"

"Friends? Liar! Ye have no friends. And no right to send her away without me knowing!"

"She's safe, James, she is. I would never do anything to harm her!"

"I'm her father! She should be here… with me!"

"You! You hit her!" she screamed, and he lashed out again in rage. Suddenly she stopped, very still. "You will *never* find her," she said quietly. "Never! She has gone into the bush. No – *now* she is safe!"

He swore. "Gone scrub – like a black-fella savage? Oh, ye have done it now! Once a convict! Always a convict. I'll see to it! Ye are going back! Back!" He dragged on the rope, her hands burning down the cable as she tried to ease off the tension.

"James! James! I am free. I have my ticket! I have. I've done my time! "

"Free? You are not free. There is no Ticket..." His eyes narrowed slightly.

But she did not see. "It came through when you were away. You know my time is done. James, I'm free! We can build the life we always dreamed of... we can." She pulled at the collar on her neck, her hands weak from exhaustion of the constant battle. She felt her strength to fight ebb away – the tide was against her. She was losing. Under her breath, in the desperation of being washed out to sea, she screamed in her head. *"Oh God! Lord Jesus! Help me! Save me! I need you to fight for me! Please God!"* No longer did she question her right to ask. No longer did she worry that she did not deserve it. Her prayer book said God is the defender of the weak. She had no answers to the injustice that was tugging at her hair and her throat, only that God would never withhold his mercy from anyone. She pleaded for Him to come and fight her cause, tears stinging her prayer on its way.

James looked at her, openly calculating and cold, contempt oozing from the snarl on his lip. "Ticket?" he repeated. "I've never seen any ticket."

"Yes..." she sobbed.

His eyes narrowed again. "I don't believe ye!"

"It's true. I have it... I'll show you. It's true. Release the collar. Please. I'll show you."

"Show me first – ye liar!" He jerked the rope again and pulled her off balance. "Now!"

A faint glimmer of hope registered in her green eyes. Yes... she would show him. Then he would know. She struggled to her feet and made her way to the crude bush sideboard. She pushed it aside and ran her fingers down the mud-daub wall. She felt for a crack and worked out a small brick that was part of the wall. She lifted out a box, dust falling away as she opened the lid and folded out the contents. She placed it on the table. It was a document with the Governor's seal: a ticket of pardon. It was true. She lifted her chin, wearing her shackles with elegance. She was free, and suddenly she realised this was an internal liberty, just as much as the document before her gave her freeman status. Gartery looked at her. She returned his stare steadily.

He picked up the thick paper. "This is yer ticket? Mrs Polly Gartery..." he read. "Amazing..." She allowed herself a gentle smile then. She hadn't realised he didn't know. It made such a difference. One piece of paper...

But he turned on her again. "Fool! Ye think this changes anything? Do ye? Once a convict!" he snarled. "It doesn't matter what this upstart Scot thinks he can write on paper... it doesn't change the *facts*!" He screwed up the paper very slowly and dragged her out the back. Smouldering embers under the large cast iron pot smoked and hissed wearily as a fine drizzle misted down. He tossed it onto the ashes. "Ye ain't got a prayer Polly! Ya got nothing!"

"Noo! Oh no!" She screamed, pulling at the rope, groping powerlessly into the air to save the document. The edges curled black apologetically. The ink on the charred paper turned silver as the fire burnt her freedom away. "Nooo…" she cried sobbing hysterically as she fell onto her knees, her nails scraping towards her freedom, and he yanked the rope harder.

* * *

5.

The girls followed Percy as he led them across country. They were intrigued. Where was he taking them? The excursion was not entirely in keeping with a rough possum-hunter.

"Where is Burilda?" asked Jo. Percy picked up his bushman's pace, smoothly walking though scrub as if it was a blazed highway. Jo easily kept up, tucking her skirt up out of the way unashamedly. Andi and Jane came puffing and panting behind.

"She's gone ahead. We'll meet later."

"Where are we going?" Jane tugged on his sleeve as he paused so they could catch up.

"Just a mite further... step carefully here – it's a bit narrow," he said as they passed some rocky outcrops, along barely visible tracks. He waited where the trees cleared in a natural arch to give them a stunning view of a rugged valley below them. Andi leant wearily on a low hanging branch, trying to catch her breath, and looked over the vastness of an undisturbed world. Suddenly just like the eagle, she felt she was soaring, high above God's beautiful creation.

Even Jane stood and looked in amazement. "I've never seen anything like this before," she whispered. "It's so beautiful."

Jo rested her hand on Andi's shoulder and whispered, "Kind'a a shame it won't stay like this forever..." *Some aspects of progress*, she thought ruefully, *isn't all grand.*

But Percy was not one to dilly-dally, and soon they were off again, winding down towards the valley. Their energy quickly focused on the job of keeping up. Andi almost became frantic in case she lost sight of those ahead. She knew what it was like to really be lost. She swiped the perspiration off her face and tugged at her long skirt, which constantly snagged on brush as she went.

Then suddenly – as if he read her thoughts, he stopped. He turned the good side of his face to the girls and closed his eye. "Listen – we're nearly there…" The girls closed their eyes too, listening. A low rumble echoed around the valley that became more distinct as they focused on it. "Ya ready? Nearly lunch time," announced Percy and he headed off again.

The girls followed, curiosity bubbling up as the rumble became louder and louder… and they couldn't be sure, but under the deep thunderous roar it almost sounded like there were yells and squeals of laughter. The next turn, around some large rocks and the valley floor opened wide in a clearing.

A waterfall boomed over a rock-face, crashing underneath into a clear wide pool of the deepest blue, reflecting the sky above. Tree ferns, creepers, and orchids with large sprays of flowers grew in a perpetual greenhouse of fine mist. But what the girls noticed first was the children – laughing and splashing, calling, and diving, showing off in pure fun. Their wet naked bodies glistened as the sunlight broke through the clouds. They chased and swam and splashed, hollering with delight while their laughter echoed around the rock walls of their Eden.

Jo did not pause. "I'm in!" she called, "Come on – this is fantastic!" She striped off to her underwear and dived straight in. Andi hesitated. She glanced at the few adult women sitting patiently around the edges of the rock pools, hand twisting rope from piles of grass beside them; others weaving and tying string bags. Jane looked bewildered. There were so many children... and they were all naked.

Percy nudged them. "Don't you like getting your feet wet?" he asked.

Andi didn't know what to say. "I don't have swimming-togs... or a towel... or anything. That's all."

Percy figured Sterling ways didn't matter here. "Can't say I can see anyone else with whatever they are. Jo's got the right idea in my mind," he laughed.

Andi looked at Jane and smiled encouragingly. "It's so hot – why don't we?" She slipped off her skirts and dangled her toes in the water. It was cold – refreshing and clean. They edged their way in. As the water crept to their knees they were gasping as the coolness stole over their hot sweaty skin.

Suddenly they looked up. Dozens of bright brown eyes were staring at them curiously. Everyone stood quietly. Jo was sitting on a rock not far away... her cotton under-clothes clinging to her body. Andi reached out and held Jane's hand reassuringly. Suddenly she was back with the Green Team facing unknown terrors of the night. "Guess they have not seen many girls with clothes on before," she whispered to Jane. She looked around at Percy, who was whittling a piece of driftwood, apparently unaware of the spectacle they had created.

Jo stood up. Andi held her breath, and Jane blinked her puffy lid eyes. No one moved. Jo raised her hands above her head, bent her knees, jumped high and somersaulted in the air. She bombed an entry that sent a tsunami to the edges of the waterhole. The kids squealed as the water kicked up hard in their faces. One boy looked unimpressed and squared his shoulders. He copied Jo's questionable style and created a far more spectacular splash. Jo clapped his efforts with a laugh.

Suddenly the scene was reactivated, and their enjoyment resumed with vigour. Little children swam over and tugged at Andi's clothes. She smiled at their inquisitive prodding, and she allowed them to touch her fair skin, and her unusual hair, as they tried to determine if it was some sort of trick.

* * *

James roughly tugged at the rope. The noonday sun steamed up small muddy puddles left over from the drizzly night. Heat reflected in hazy waves off the bare ground around the settlement. "Ye ain't got a prayer, Polly Gartery. I'm gunna sell ye – like the cow ya are. Only difference bein' thar' bony old cow would bring a fairer price." He dragged her along, the collar rubbing the skin around her neck raw. He jerked at the rope when her pace lagged, and she was forced to stumble on at his bidding.

She no longer struggled or begged. Her head was weak from the heat and exhaustion. She just whispered prayers… prayers to her Father-God, asking for his protection over Jane. She had no way of knowing if she had met up with Percy… if she was safe… but she prayed. She was not left powerless yet. James was wrong – she did have a prayer.

He made his way to the wharf, stopping as he came upon various acquaintances asking of anyone who may have use for a discarded woman. He had shaved his beard and combed his hair. Polly had been given no toileting liberties. Her dishevelled appearance belied her ability and poise. She closed her eyes against the glare. She no longer looked at the faces that traded her like stock. Less actually. In this colony, cattle in any condition brought a good price.

A disinterested voice mentioned, "Them at the corner are looking for 'help'. No one knows why – they've got more than their fair share already." The news showed promise and James pulled Polly down to the quayside. Her dress snagged, tripping her in her weak, fragile state. He dragged her to her feet cursing, his rough hands ripping her dress at the bodice. She clutched the fragments together as he tugged her along. He had just one item on his agenda: to rid himself of this total humiliation. He cursed the day he caught the eye of a tall, elegant convict and thought life would be different in the new world. Yeah, it was different. It was tougher, more biased, more prejudiced than he ever imagined. There would never be room for him to move while she was here. After today, she no longer existed.

"Ah, Mr Thornton, I heard youse was looking for house-help. I got no use for this 'un, and me was counting on ya bein' inclined to take her."

George looked distastefully at the sailor. He was rough as bags under his clean uniform. "I think our situation is satisfactory as it is."

"Oh, but Harry back there told me ya was looking to get some help. Now I knows she looks a mess but she scrubs up okay. And she can cook and clean like a trouper…." James tugged her around so that he could see her bruised face.

George Thornton smiled shrewdly. "If she's so jolly good, why would you relinquish her services?"

"I'm on duty with Her Majesty's fleet. It just don't suit me to have her. Practical issues my good man… practical issues." James swallowed and thought longingly about the casket of rum he stashed under the bed at the hut. He almost wished he had made her clean up and put on another dress. Embarrassing – the way she stood there clutching at herself like she cared. Whore!

Thornton turned away disinterested. "My wife's not available just now. It would depend on her."

James grinned then – with all the contempt he could muster. "You are bidden to ya missus then? Ye one of them types that got no backbone to make a decision regarding his own? Well, it figures…" and he turned to leave in disgust. Some onlookers gave a derogatory snigger in agreement.

Mr Thornton stood up straight. His chin lifted. "Well, no. That's not the way of it at all."

"Aye. But ye figure those who works under *your* roof is no concern of yours?" James raised a sceptical eyebrow to the comrades of solidarity who had started to gather around him. "I guess not…" and another round of mirth trickled from the onlookers.

George looked uncomfortable. He could see what was happening. He had no interest in women's affairs. He rightly left all that to Eliza, but his hand was being forced by public opinion, and public opinion mattered to George Thornton. He swore. He needed to nip this quickly before it escalated. "Very well then. I'll take her."

But James was not finished. "Well, Mr Thornton, we don' wanna put ya missus out. She might be want'n a say!" This time the laughter was blatantly humiliating.

"Give her over, or I leave. I have matters to attend to!" He reached out to take the rope.

James held it firmly. "Without a finders-fee, for finding ya quality help? That'd not be gentlemanly like, would it be Mr Thornton?" The unified agreement around the fringes was unyielding. "Sterling would be in keepin' with providing ye with sterling service," he added slyly. His price had gone up. George looked at the rabble. They were becoming edgy.

"You scoundrel! You're no better than a thieving convict yourself!" He dug in his pocket and pulled out a combination of some English shillings, Dutch Guilders, and a Holey dollar – a Spanish coin that had the centre punched out, used to address the currency shortage in the colony. "Here! Take it..." He flung them on the ground in disgust and hurriedly led her away to escape the common rabble.

* * *

The late afternoon sun cast deep shadows onto the rocky walls curtained with fern fronds behind them. Mist from the waterfall blew cool air over them and the water gurgled around their feet as it made its way down stream. The girls sat on the rocks, picking white meat from the bones of fresh-water fish that had been cooked wrapped in leaves.

Roasted nuts were shared around too. "Everything belongs to everyone," Percy said. It spoke volumes.

"Did Burilda leave again?" asked Andi looking around.

He nodded. He was unperturbed by her comings and goings. "We'll make camp not far from here since it's getting late. Burilda will meet us there." He picked up some spears and hunting weapons and carried them comfortably as one who is familiar with the tools of his trade. They left then, the girls waving their farewells to the few adults who remained after the picnic had dispersed.

* * *

6.

Percy quickly lit a fire as the last glow on the horizon was fading. Large basalt boulders sheltered their camp. Lichen clung to it in spidery patterns that leapt and danced in the firelight. The girls sat side by side, their backs against the natural rock walls, reaching their chilled hands into the warmth of the orange flames. "I left my shawl at the other camp," sighed Jane.

"Burilda will grab it. She should be here soon," said Percy. "Here come in closer to the fire."

"Isn't it kinda late, for her to be out alone in the bush?" asked Andi shivering. She remembered being alone in the bush at night.

Percy shook his head. "This is Burilda. The bush is her pantry, her cook-house, and her parlour. There's not one bit she don't know about it... and what she don't know – I figure it ain't needed. Aye – she knows her way 'round all right..." He paused then. "I asked her to get the mash for your eye Miss Jane. It would do well with her tendin' it."

Jane shuddered involuntarily. "No! I don't want my eye to pop out."

"Pop out?" Jo looked at her quizzically.

"Yeah... witch-doctor stuff. It'll make my eye... you know..."

"Oh," said Percy nodding seriously with a frown. The talk of ignorance and fear was loud. "You reckon that's what happened to my eye?"

Jane startled and cringed back away from the fire. She had made him angry. Would he hit her? But he didn't move, looking deep into the embers at the base of the fire. Always he faced his good eye towards them now. He waited. "Is it?" he repeated.

Jane stammered, swallowed, and muttered, "I dunno."

Jo looked at Percy's profile in the flame light. His hair and beard were wild and unkempt, yet underneath, there was a sensitive twist on his mouth and something about his fine chiselled nose made you think he was more than an ex-con possum-hunter. "What happened to your eye?" Jo asked. She'd been dying to ask.

He turned his face around, giving them full view of the palsied lid. The eye twisted unnaturally around in a grotesque stare. He started to speak and then stopped as Andi turned away and covered her mouth. What was he thinking? They were only girls. They didn't need to know the hideous details of his unfortunate life.

He moved back out of the firelight and turned his malformed eye away. Perhaps it was time to relinquish that torturous oath he had made. He made a pledge that he would inflict on the world the ordeal of having to look at the deformed results of his trauma. That's why he never wore a patch. He knew his face was hideous… but *he* didn't have to look at it. They did. That was the price they had to pay for doing this to him. They took part in all the barbarianism of this place, and every time he saw the flicker of revulsion cross the faces of those he met, he thought they deserved it. But he didn't count on the wounds in his soul being ripped open again and again, by their stares.

Perhaps this is what Grandma Hetty meant… perhaps now was the time to move on. Perhaps it *was* time to wear a patch. He reached up and ran a finger down the raised scar tissue of his face. Even now, it was sensitive if he rubbed it in a certain way. Sometimes he would touch it – just like pressing a bruise to see if it was still tender… but it was always the same. He winced and glanced at the girls who were now staring at him expectantly.

"Ya don' need to know…" he mumbled.

"True," conceded Jo, "but it would help Jane to know it wasn't Burilda's medicine that did that."

"Aye." Jane looked so much like her mother as she tried to keep her head up and disappear into the shadows at the same time. He saw fear creeping into her little face. "Okay… It's like this. I got my pardon and afterwards… that same day – I was ambushed. Some brave individuals bashed me around the head to remind me of my place," he said sarcastically. "I took to the bush and got away. But I was in such a bad way I collapsed. The men from Burilda's mob found me and took me back to their camp. Burilda was given the job to take care of me. They didn't expect me to live, and I nearly died a few times, but she kept nursin' me back. By the time I came round, Burilda was already considered my woman. They made me part of the tribe. Their initiation is nothing compared to the treatment I'd had when I came here. I remember I looked at an officer the wrong way once. He ordered 50 lashes on the spot. Just for lookin'." He shook his head; even now he couldn't comprehend it. But he pursed his lips staunchly. "They didn't win, ya know. If ye don't go under – they don't win."

"There you go Jane," said Andi. "Burilda's medicine helped save Percy's life. That's good."

Jane was rather sceptical. It didn't look very good. She shook her head and grunted.

Jo was thoughtful. "Burilda's tribe adopted you? But you're 'white'!"

He nodded, "I'm white… but I'm no colonial. The elders say we have the same enemies… because white-fellas nearly killed me. That makes us brothers." He sighed and looked deep into the settling coals of the fire. To have an aboriginal woman, who wasn't *forced* to be with a white man, was pretty much an unknown thing. Yet Burilda was the best thing that had happened to him. Not many people had stuck by him in his life. Even Annie, his English girl, had dropped him like a hotcake when push came to shove. His mother had died of a fever and his dad worked like a Trojan to support his seven children. Although he knew his parents had no choice to leave like that, in his little boy heart it still felt like desertion.

It was Grandma Hetty who filled the gap. They always called her Grandma Hetty. For such a little lady, the name Henrietta seemed too big for her. Yet there was nothing else about her that was small. She had a huge heart. Percy never doubted that Grandma Hetty loved him. She was one of the faithful ones. He pictured her, apron ties flapping and her little wiry face glowing with sweat as she bucketed out watery stew for his young brothers and sisters, making it go the distance.

Yet she never complained. Those years should have been her time to kick back and reap the harvest of her mature years. She always said, "God gave me two families to be raisin', 'cause He knew in his wisdom, I woulda bin lost without ya's all." So, Grandma Hetty worked and worked, and sometimes when Percy would come in from his late-night carousing, he'd find her asleep at the table out of sheer exhaustion, her little Bible open at her elbow.

One night he came in and found her dozing. He went to tiptoe around her as he normally did, but she sat bolt upright and stuck out her little knobbly boot so he went sprawling on the floor. She was only little but she was made of tough stuff. She picked him up and sat him at the table like a nursery-child. "Percival son, you give me more grief than the rest of this clan put together. I bin praying for ya soul, and I don't like the direction ya goin'."

He said nothing. He didn't like disappointing Grandma Hetty, but she was old, and she didn't live in the real world – with her Bible and her prayers and all. As he looked back, he wasn't sure how he thought that caring for seven grandkids and an overworked, underpaid son, didn't give her a grip on reality. But back then she had seemed sheltered. He was young and bold and angry. Poaching served the two-fold purpose. It provided much needed money and food, not that Grandma Hetty would have a bar of it, if she thought it was not "kosher". Percy was first-rate at spinning a good yarn, convincing her what he presented was all above board. And then, poaching was a way of getting even with the gentry-establishment. Getting even was a grand cause: they had way too much anyway.

Grandma Hetty handed him a warm drink and sat down opposite him. "Ya bin boozing again," she observed. She didn't seem to like him any less for it, but he remembers her crinkled brow squeezing together tightly in the candlelight. Son, I gunna say this once and then I gunna leave it. But I needs to say it once. I's bin praying for ya, Percy. I bin praying, 'cause you are heavy on my soul. And the Good Lord done showed me some things... and they are scaring me mighty. He's tellin' me you're going to destroy yourself... nearly, but not quite. God in His mercy will pull ya back from the brink and you'll remember your training, and you'll become a man of influence: a Godly man of influence." Grandma Hetty had tears streaming down her wrinkled cheeks, but she didn't stop. "A Godly man of influence... that is what I'm hanging on tight for you Perce. And whatever does come, you remember two things son: ya Grandma-Hetty loves you and so does your Father God in Heaven. And there will come a time when you need to patch things over and move on... the rest He'll see to Himself." She stood up then and left for her bed.

True to her word she never mentioned it again, but those words were branded on his soul. Even as he stood in the wooden dock, with that hard judge carelessly presiding over his life, Grandma Hetty's five-foot-nothing frame stood tall and proud, clutching her chest like she did with the little ones every morning before they went out the door. "You might be going out to into the world, my darlings, but I got you tight in here," she would whisper. "I got you tight in here."

* * *

Percy looked up from his reverie. The girls were crumpled together in an exhausted heap. He rubbed his brow with his calloused hand. It baffled him still. How could one little old woman across the other side of the world have so much influence? Influence! He almost wanted to laugh. It was a ridiculous thing...what she had said that night... that *he* could – would – be a man of influence. Then he remembered that was only half the story... the other half was "Godly". He laughed again, this time out loud. That was even more ridiculous than the first. How could he be anything other than the poacher, the deserted, the condemned, the convict, the scarred, the shunned?

He stirred up the coals in the fire with a stick and stared as the sparks flew and swirled up into the inky night. A faint glow from the disturbed fire fell on the girls' faces sleeping under his protection. He looked on them bemused, as the glow seemed to move over and swell in his chest. *Grandma Hetty*, he thought affectionately, *she loved me. She believed in me. She said God loved me too. Ha!* He threw a small stick into the fire and a shower of sparks funnelled up into the sky. What evidence was there of that? How had God ever shown him he was loved?

You'll remember your training. He did remember the family Bible as it sat dusted and careful on the shelf behind the table. His dad would take it down and read a passage after a meal when he was home. Deep in the flames there swelled and swirled the patterns of fire. A picture formed in the energy of the coals. It was of one man, tortured and drawn, strung out tight as he suffered a flogging. As the picture moved into life, he felt the lashes cut into his back again. He relived the agony of the whip and the scorn of his captors and the loneliness of desertion. But then, the picture rotated and the face on the image was not his; it was the face of one in the family Bible: the face of Jesus. A whisper from within the glow in his heart spoke... *"You suffered because you were justly condemned; I suffered because I love you. Man has no greater love than this – than to lay down his life for his brother."*

Percy sat still for a long time, not daring to move. He wanted evidence of God's love? An innocent man suffered when he didn't have to, so he could go free! It was a faultless analogy for him – the natural world around him representing the spiritual world he could not see, in a way he understood very well...too well. The lessons of his boyhood, things he had discarded as useless, came flooding in. One after another, he saw how God was demonstrating his love.

But when the scenes stopped rolling, another vision came. It was of a hand that was about to write his ticket of pardon...but it stopped and pushed the paper aside. Percy curled his lip then. Cynicism darkened his face. Of course, there would be a catch... of course it would not end in freedom. That would be too perfect.

Percy took a breath and held it – somehow, he desperately needed to know if this dream of freedom – real freedom, was possible. He let out a relieved breath, as the hand that held the quill again moved... to scribe his name on the pardon. But then, as if disappointment was inevitable, the hand scratched out his name and threw it away. Percy's face turned to ash, tears pouring from his good eye. Was life always a conglomerate of disappointment and trampled dreams? *God? Where are you? Was Grandma Hetty a fool after all, to believe?* At that very moment the same hand produced a new document: a certificate. Although Percy could read only elementary letters, he knew that this official document represented something far more significant. It said he had been *born* free! A whole new life was created, with no records, no history, no scars. The seal at the bottom was made in blood. Percival Holmes was a Free Man, not an emancipated one!

With the sincerity of a child, he knelt just as he had seen Grandma Hetty do every day of his boyhood. He prayed simply. Grandma Hetty was right – it was *time to patch things over and move on.* It couldn't get plainer than that. She liked things plain and straight, Grandma Hetty did.

* * *

7.

Polly stared over her shoulder at James in disbelief as the man led her away. She hadn't registered name or place while the trade progressed. Her mind screamed with humiliation and injustice blotting out details. She did not care to know with who or where she was going. She just needed to go back home. She needed to find Jane. She needed her life back. All those years, the paying out her debt to an unmerciful law, and now the evidence of that work was gone – all gone. Everyone had heard the Governor's Cryer make known the general Emancipist's Clause. She remembered every word of it with fear:

> *"His Excellency, the Governor, will bear no excuse of Freedom Pardons, either Absolute or Conditional, or Tickets of Leave, as being lost or mislaid: and such persons as shall not produce these Documents will be considered as Prisoners, and recalled to Government Public Labour."*

James had not burnt a piece of paper – he had extinguished her life. Her normal bold and articulate self was reduced to this. She blinked her lashes hard, the swelling of the bruises about her face stinging as salty tears washed over them.

* * *

James watched her go with a satisfied sneer. He pushed back his shoulders as he felt those around him pat his back, and he loudly celebrated his freedom from the burden of being tied to the lower class. It never occurred to him that those who congratulated him were on the very same level of the food chain. The only difference was that they doggedly lived in the delusion that in some way they were better than run-of-the-mill scum.

James enjoyed this camaraderie. It felt good to be a leader instead of always being the one taking orders: the seaman, the underling. "I've got me a little girl to find. My little girl…" A wheeze caught in his throat; it burned with desire for rum. But it sounded like the emotion of a distraught father. "I gotta save her from bein' used like a dog… a slave…" he said indignantly. The story added even more tragedy to a family man coming home from empirical duty for the British Crown to find his family in tatters. He adjusted his respectable coat. It also gave credibility to his plight.

"Poor kid…"

"It ain't right…."

"Whatever ya need…"

"We're here for ye…"

"Tell us what we can do…"

It was the only time in their short unfortunate lives where injustice had spurred this rabble on to right a wrong. They had no idea who James was, yet they rallied around him as a brother. Within half an hour he had a fully armed lynch mob ready to do his bidding.

Polly had said Jane was safe in the Bush. James was not dumb. She had to *be* with someone. The visiting trader perhaps? That was the only outsider she ever mentioned. And it wouldn't be far. They wouldn't take a girl – a white girl, deep into that inhospitable bush. He told them what he knew... like puzzle pieces laid out on the table.

A man stepped forward with a sinister glint in his eyes. James watched him eyeing the ale jug like a predator. "Me name is Strapper. I'm thinking that I might be able to help. Worked with a trapper once. Bastard of a bloke... he was known for getting in with the locals. Nothing would be below him. He had some favourite spots..." Strapper gave him a toothless grin.

So, fate smiled on James, and he smiled back. He rewarded Strapper with round of rum. He downed his tankard and then he went back for another. This time the tables were turned. Jane would be close; she would come to Daddy, and justice would be served.

* * *

Polly stood, clutching her torn dress dazed, unheeding her surroundings, her red hair falling about her face in a dirty, scruffy tangle. George tried to explain her to his wife. "Honestly Eliza the man gave me no choice. Anyway, I can't see the harm in having her here... you have mentioned more than once we were needing extra help."

"Oh George – look at her! She is obviously from the streets.... or the caves! You've heard of those destitute creatures that live in caves like rats.... I really don't think it's a good idea. Just think what sort of problem she could be!"

"Now Eliza, don't get hysterical. I won't turn her out. Not now. Call someone and get her cleaned up." His tone wavered between pacifying and commanding action. He wasn't just going to turn her out when he'd paid money, *good* money for her service. He didn't want his wife becoming stubborn over the issue. It was done, and that was that. "I'll go down and see what I can find out tomorrow. There'll be some record on when she arrived and how. We'll know more then."

Bridget was summoned. She came in, a grin constantly playing around her lips. She wore respectable plain clothes, and a maidly cotton cap that didn't have a hope of containing her unruly mop of hair. Mrs Thornton spoke in a resigned voice. She wearied of constantly trying to make Bridget understand the decorum she required. "Bridget, take this woman and fix her up. Assist her toilet and tend her hair. There will be clothes from Miriam's wardrobe that will do until something can be found for her later."

Mrs Thornton turned to go when she heard Bridget emit a ghastly cry. She pursed her lips. "Spare me the dramatics", she said, pausing to draw an exaggerated deep and patient breath. "I know the woman is a mess! That is why I need her cleaned up!" she said sharply. "Girl, will you ever learn to just do what is requested? I should dock your earnings, just to help you understand!"

Eliza glanced back, more rebukes on her tongue when there seemed no response, but she stopped – astonished. Bridget was kneeling before the pathetic woman who was totally oblivious to her attentions. Bridget had tears in her eyes, tenderly sobbing. "Oh Mrs Gartery, what happened to ye? Oh Ma'am! Whoever did this dreadful thing?"

* * *

Before the shafts of early dawn shone onto the ground, they blundered through the scrub, made brave by the amber ale that James had passed around the hut during the nightlong vigil. Strapper followed obscure signs of bush traffic, his basic tracking gave the men a direction, a place to start. Whether it was an indication of man or beast – they had no idea, but Strapper spurred them on, believing they were hot on the trail like finely trained bloodhounds.

They burst into the clearing around the coachwood tree as the grey morning lightened. They stared in silent disbelief at the evidence of a recent fire; the tall flask and sack that had carried the flour from the house; recently eaten meals; a stray button and the bark shelter. Even James was sobered by the reality that Jane had really been here, as he poked in the cold ashes.

A low whistle caught his attention and he looked up. Lying asleep in the shadows of the gunya lay Burilda, her pregnant body heavy with tiredness. A fresh collection of berries and leaves lay in the shallow bark Coolamon dish beside her. Under her head was the meagre luxury of Jane's folded shawl.

As if awakened by ghosts Burilda started to her feet, her pregnant body strangely sluggish and unresponsive. She stared in horror at the angry mob that surrounded her bed. She never knew who they were and what they wanted. They needed no reason to deal out a violent payback for a crime that was never committed. They left the scene without remorse, nursing a frustrating sense that an inadequate justice had been served.

As they trudged back to the hut, James was relieved. He never thought about what he would do with Jane if they actually found her. Maybe sell her to some isolated recluse. But he needn't think about the girl now. Fortune was finally smiling on him – finally after years of injustice. He would skip the navy for a merchant ship. Conveniently *The Helena* was already docked in the harbour. She was leaving the day after tomorrow for the Caribbean. Such a venture would symbolise his new freedom.

* * *

Percy stirred in the early morning light. A glossy, black crow sat on a low branch, cawing a long mournful moan, the wind ruffling the feathers around its neck. A strange sense of tragedy disturbed his sleep. He sat up and threw a rock at the bird. Its mournful cry was a dirge song to a tribesman, and he had a strong dislike for their desolate wail. Percy piled some small sticks on the fire, stirring the ashes into life. He looked around and was quietly surprised that Burilda was not here yet. He knew there would be reason enough. He shook off the morose feeling as he grabbed his spear and disappeared into the trees. Shortly he returned with some fat forest pigeons and proceeded to make breakfast.

He remembered last night and took a deep breath. Perhaps that accounted for this feeling that was disturbing his spirit. If nothing else Percy was stubborn, and having made a choice, he determined to see it through. He never really understood before that you could be stubborn about good things. Grandma Hetty often despaired over his stubborn heart, but he nodded as he realised that he would need it now more than ever. For some reason he understood that if life was hard before, it had just got harder.

"Oh God, give me courage to stick at this," he prayed. Of all the people he knew, it was the ones who quit that he despised most. He toed the girls in the side to rouse them for breakfast. He didn't know anyone to sleep as soundly as these three, out here in the bush. "Breakfast…" he announced, and then he looked straight at Andi. "I would be like'n ya help, if you're think'n you could manage it."

They ate breakfast promptly, their curiosity stirred by such an odd request. He held up his knife. "How about it, Miss Andi?"

Andi stood quite still. "Knives aren't really one of my strong points," she confessed. She had no idea what Percy had in mind. But he seemed to waver, so she relented. "Okay… as long as I don't have to kill anything – I am definitely worse with dead things."

He handed her the knife. "I be want'n a haircut," he said regaining his boldness. "You seem to be the one who does things with hair," he said, indicating her fringe.

Jo stood up immediately. "A haircut? Really? You want Andi to give you a haircut… with a skinning knife?" She burst out laughing. The picture of Andi hairdressing with a machete was too much to take seriously!

Percy regarded her seriously. "I'm not think'n its funny. I'm need'n a change. What is so ticklish about that?"

Jo shook her head and laughed even more.

Andi looked dubious. "Don't you have scissors?"

Percy frowned. "For cutting hair? This 'ere is the sharpest blade around."

Andi stood over him; knife poised like she was enacting a dramatic scene in a Shakespearian tragedy. "How? I mean – how do you want it?"

"I don't know. Me thinkin' doin' hair is what girls is good at."

Jo grunted, "Sure, but you have to do it with that thing!"

Andi looked curiously at his matted head. "It's a poor craftsman who blames his tools," she said philosophically. She was entrusted with an enormous responsibility, and she took it very seriously. She turned to Jane for advice. "What do you reckon Jane? How do other men around town do their hair? Do we go pony-tail, side-burns, short-back-and-sides?"

"Mohawk," suggested Jo helpfully.

Andi ignored her and picked up some hair, testing it on the knife. It cut easily. Percy was right about his knife being sharp. A plan was forming in her head. She set to work, one section at a time, cutting carefully, totally focused on her sculpture. Every so often, she'd paused and ask Jane, "So what do you think?" She'd offer an occasional suggestion.

"Do you think Burilda will like your new look?" asked Jo, feeling a little cut out of this process.

"We will find out soon enough – no doubt," said Percy eyeing the fallen masses of matted hair that encrusted the ground about the log where he sat. Perhaps this was taking the whole thing too far. Surely God wouldn't be wantin' him to go berserk. Perhaps an eye-patch would be enough.

Suddenly Andi dropped the knife and it fell upright, twanging into the log. "Ahhh!" she screamed. She jumped back shaking, her face washed out as if she had seen a phantom. "It moved!" she whispered shakily.

Percy leaped up, swiped the knife in one fluid movement, spinning around on the defensive. "Where!" he hissed, scanning the ground for the offending creature.

Andi pointed to his head. "It moved..." she repeated with a tremble. Head lice. Eww.

Jo covered her mouth with her hand, and turned away, also shaking. It was too much! But she couldn't hold it in and burst out laughing. "You said you're not good with dead things. Not too good with live ones either it seems!" Andi glared at Jo for her indiscretion.

Percy looked at her suspiciously. He handed the knife-blade back to her by the handle. "Oh – that's all..." he said unconcerned, scratching his scalp. "Well, they ain't gunna eat ya, now are they?" He sat back down and waved for her to resume.

She couldn't stop her hands shaking. Suddenly she felt wriggling all over her scalp, and she tried not to scratch. How do you get rid of these sorts of nasty critters without a pharmacy full of bottles of shampoos and lotions?

Jo looked at Percy enjoying this spectacle immensely. He sat with one half of his head now tidy and sculptured like a respectable looking merchant, the other – the side of his face with the sightless eye, was still wild and unruly – the crazy, rough recluse. "Most people have their hair done the same on both sides," said Jo helpfully.

Percy already regretted handing over the aesthetics of his decision, into the hands of three girls. He only wanted a haircut – swift and painless. How hard could it be? "Look," he said impatiently, "just get it done… or I'll leave it like this! Then ye'll have to look at it forever, just to remind ye of your stupidity!" Percy's jaw went firm, and he sighed. He regretted the retort. This exercise was supposed to indicate that he was moving on from such an oath; not making up new versions of it. 'Oh God…he prayed, *please be forgiving me.*

Andi's jaw dropped. "Sorry. Someone else does my hair. I haven't done this before."

He softened. "No, I be the one that's sorry. You're doin' a fine job, and I thank ye. I'm not good at bein' social… but I need to get better. Please, will ye forgive me?"

Andi stared at him. Something had changed. "Sure," and she dived into his livestock infested scalp before he changed his mind. The threat of looking at this half-finished job forever, couldn't have been a more effective incentive. Andi liked things to be completed properly.

Finally, she stood back and looked at the transformed man in front of her. His beard was trimmed and even, his hair had a natural wave that sat civilly where it was put, and he had a small ponytail at the back. Andi thought it looked very distinguished. He cleared his throat and he stood back out of the way. "Don't worry about the critters," he said reassuring Andi. "A rinse with ordinary vinegar and lamp oil will do the trick. Burilda has a concoction of red grevillea and tea tree, but mine is simpler. Check each other later and we'll do you all if we need to," he added generously.

Percy unlaced one of his boots. He slung the long leather thonging over his shoulder while he cut out a circle from a pelt. With his knife he shaved off the fur, leaving a piece of pliable rawhide. He cut two slits in the patch and threaded the leather lace through it. The girls watched as he tied the two stands of leather about his head and adjusted the patch by sliding it over his sightless eye. It wasn't comfortable, but if this was what he needed to do, he would get used to it.

* * *

Eliza Thornton sat in her morning parlour opposite Polly. She looked at her bemused. Even though her dress was servile and simple, it was obvious the woman had grace and style. Her hair was washed and elegantly rolled on her neck. The fair skin on her face and neck was marked with red blotches and bruises. Yet Polly sat there unseeing, her chin raised, and her expression blank.

Eliza didn't quite know what to do. The woman had not spoken a word: in two days – nothing. She could ask one of the doctors to pay a visit, but there didn't seem anything much wrong with her physically apart from a few bruises. She'd heard of this sort of thing happening, and she was concerned.

Eliza was none too swayed by Bridget's distressed reunion with her previous mistress. Bridget was always a drama queen, but she carefully watched how Miriam reacted. Miriam was sensible and able to manage the work of three girls. The girl's face had drained of its colour, she ran and got a basin of water and loosened that degrading collar from around her neck. Within half an hour the lady had her dignity restored and was requested by Miriam to allow her lady full bed rest.

Miriam whole-heartedly believed Mrs Thornton had intentionally rescued Mrs Gartery from the depths of humiliation. Miriam responded with a warmer manner and greater industry than ever before. Eliza happily allowed the misconception to persist. Servants and convicts talked. In a small colony, it was best to say nothing. Eliza was well aware that by her silence she could emerge from this awkward situation a heroine.

'That is fine,' Eliza thought to herself as she poured a cup of tea in the parlour, *'but what do I do with her in the meantime? She can't hold a spoon, much less do anything useful.'* Her silence had cornered Mrs Thornton into a benevolence she did not feel. It was very important that the gold stars kept coming. They outweighed the inconvenience or even the expense. This was the solitary common characteristic that sustained their marriage. Both Mr and Mrs Thornton lived for gold star endorsements.

She called for Bridget to take Mrs Gartery back to her bed, and dispatched a message to the surgeon-general, to attend their house at his convenience.

* * *

Percy strode ahead. The feeling inside his chest had grown more intense as the morning progressed. He couldn't understand it. Where was God's promise of peace? If he had aligned himself with the purposes of the cosmic God of the universe, why did he feel like his chest was about to explode? Or implode. He stopped and turned to face the girls.

"I gotta confess to ya's. I prayed last night. I prayed that God would forgive me stubbornness and make me His own, so now He's made me a free-born. I'm God's own." There – he said it. Confessing before a person, that was important. At least, he thought it was. These girls were the only people he had access to. So, that should do it. He stood there waiting for the peace to return. It didn't. He was surprised by the jubilation on Andi's face, the respect that lit Jo's eyes and the relief wash over Jane... but inside... inside – it was no different. *Blast it all! It's gotta make a difference – or what's the point?*

He suppressed agonised groan from deep within as he sat down. "I ain't goin' nowhere now – until God shows me it makes a difference!" He sat cross-legged like a tribesman... and waited. Jo shook her head as they stood back and watched him... waiting. He could be here forever... like Henny Penny... waiting for the sky to fall in.

For three hours he sat there and did not move. The girls were listless and impatient to get moving. To go where and to do what exactly, did not matter. They just wanted to get "going".

"You'd better pray," suggested Jo quietly after she had picked and shredded every leaf in her vicinity, "that God gives him what he needs, or we'll fossilize right here beside him!" She didn't look like she would submit to such a geological process quietly.

Andi shrugged. "It's okay for you to pray too you know. I don't have special privileges."

"Maybe not. But you're more practiced at it."

Andi looked at Percy, with his hair cut and tidy, his patch sitting in place, his good eye closed. He looked every bit the new creation that God promised, but evidently it was pretty much externals for him at the moment. Slowly she began to speak. *"They that wait upon the Lord will renew their strength — they will mount up with wings like eagles, they shall run and not be weary, they shall walk and not faint."* Jane gave her a very weird look. "That's something out of the Bible. I was going to talk with my Green Girls about it…"

Jane raised her eyebrows even higher. These people were very peculiar indeed!

"It's a Girl's club. They're not actually green," explained Andi quickly. "Anyway, I don't think I've ever seen anyone really wait on God before. But Percy is actually waiting."

Jo was impatient. It didn't suit her to wait. But suddenly it occurred to her that being a friend to Percy, meant waiting *with* him, not just *for* him. In that moment she felt a sort of connection with Percy… perhaps they were starting their faith journeys together… different ways, different styles, but doing it in the way that worked for them.

Jo walked a short distance over to a tree. "God," she prayed. "Thank you for what you've done for Percy… and for me… but right now, he's looking and needing something… and I have no idea what that is… and I'm kinda thinking he doesn't know either. I know Andi says you know everything, even before we need it. I am asking that you provide whatever it is he needs." She sat down a little shaky as she felt a calm wash through her. "Thank You God," she whispered.

Percy sat waiting. He felt the turmoil of a storm raging in him and about him. It felt like that storm which had ripped through the forest and blown these girls across his path. But this time, he was being torn to shreds by the force of that big-blow. And then, when he thought he couldn't stand against it anymore, suddenly he was lifted off the ground by the cyclonic wind and dumped into the eye of the storm. Quiet enveloped his spirit. Tension ebbed away as a supernatural stillness washed over him. Relief stung his eyes as he realised God *did* make a difference. His expectations were not dashed. He is the God of Peace. He looked about and he could feel the storm raging around him still. Destruction was near at hand, so close he could reach out and touch it... but he was standing protected in the eye of the storm. He watched it rage on, basking in God's peace, drawing strength.

Eventually he knew it was time to move on. To stay was no longer waiting but avoiding... and he didn't even know what it was he didn't want to confront.

* * *

8.

As they travelled beside the creek, closer towards the coachwood tree, Percy felt reluctance tugging at his heart. Again, he stopped, and Jo rolled her eyes. This feeling was beyond his understanding. Percy had more knowledge of the bush than any other European he knew, yet now every bend was full of unseen obstacles. He felt a deep peace in his spirit, so he knew it was not fear that was holding him back, and still, he could not go ahead. "God what is it?" he prayed impatiently. "Is my life going to be so totally bizarre from now on?" It was confusing. He was not familiar enough with this new life with God to know what this meant.

"Okay… we stay here. We'll make a new camp. I don't understand… but that's the plan."

"But my shawl…" Jane objected.

"I left the water jar and flour there…." said Andi.

"We'll set up and then I'll go and get the few things we left behind. It isn't far and it won't take long. I feel there's going to be more waiting ahead girls so get used to it. But regardless, you need to stay here. Don't go wandering off. I need you to promise that."

He left them then, skirting the used track and making his way back towards the old camp, unseen through the bush.

* * *

Miriam held a silver cup of water to Mrs Gartery's lips as she sat in bed. Mrs Gartery responded vaguely. "Thank you, Mary-Jane. A drink always tastes better from a nice goblet, don't you think?" she whispered. Miriam nodded and said nothing. Mrs Gartery had been waffling deliriously on and off since she arrived.

"Ma'am, I got some nice broth. Here, let me help you with it." Miriam spooned the soup to her lips. She sipped it reluctantly.

The door opened and Bridget bundled into the room with a bounce. "Mims, I've got my chores all done! I'm ready to help you with Mrs Gartery."

Miriam shrugged. She knew the kind of help Bridget usually gave was a detailed account of her morning. Today she didn't mind. It was a relief to have Bridget's bubbly nonsense. At least it was better than the confused sad nonsense Mrs Gartery was muttering.

Bridget leaned over and spoke to Mrs Gartery in her happy lilts. "How are you today, Mrs Gartery?"

"I don't know how many garters there are today," mumbled Polly softly.

Miriam looked distressed. "I cannot be making head or tail of what she is sayin' Bridget. I've heard a jackass make more sense."

"Now don't be fretting Mims. She'll be gettin' better. You said yourself that something bad happened and it'll take a while to settle."

"But I am concerned that Mrs Thornton will not want to do this much longer. How can she be going home like this?"

"Well, we would go with her surely!"

"Are you certain? Would you give up your position that Mrs Gartery worked so hard to get for us?"

"Well, yeah. Mims, if Mrs Gartery be needing us, wouldn't you want to?"

"Yes, of course." Miriam leant over and wiped some soup off her lips with a napkin. "Would you like to sit on the terrace Ma'am? Just for a short time.

Suddenly Polly sat up, her eyes darted about anxiously. "Terrance? Oh no mother I don't want to see Terrance. Not even for a short time."

Miriam closed her eyes. This incoherent rambling was so distressing. But Bridget was not fazed at all. She gently held her hand. "Oh, but Terrance is such a nice boy. Don't you think you would like to see him?" she said.

Miriam looked at Bridget shocked. "Who is Terrance?" she mouthed silently.

Bridget shrugged. "I have no idea. But it shouldn't matter. If she wants to talk about Terrance, I'm happy to."

"Oh Bridget. You are such a baby! This is not a game. What will we do?"

Polly's glazed look focused on Miriam and she pulled away from Bridget and grabbed her arm. "Mary-Jane you are so right! This is not a game, and I will not play along! Tell Terrance when he comes that I will not see him."

Miriam looked startled. "Ho..how can I? I don't even…"

But Polly became agitated. "You must! I am not going to marry that… that… fraud!"

Miriam stood locked in the tight grip on her hand. "But Ma'am…"

"Oh, I know… you are going to remind me of those rows of silk – such an extravagant gift! And I should be so grateful! Huh!" She spat out some soup that pooled in her lower lip. Miriam patiently wiped it up.

"Silk?" Bridget's eyes widened. She had seen silk… she even had a handkerchief once, but to have *rows* of it… enough to make dresses out of it… like a true lady. Oh, that was something!

"The emerald green – I like that. Oh yes, I like it…. Mary-Jane – you said it brings out the colour in my eyes. And it will look so lovely with *my* necklace…I'll soon have my twenty-first birthday necklace… they match so perfectly. Oh, but I can't. I won't! I'll give it back. I'll take the silk back and tell Terrance I never want to see him again."

"You took it back? Oh Ma'am…" There was real disappointment in Bridget's voice. To be given such a gift and then return it – that was unimaginable.

"But Mary-Jane, you know I can only have the silk if I promise to marry him… and I could never do that. I won't! I'll return it… the others and the emerald-green. How it shines in the light. To wear that green would be like walking in jewels. It is so beautiful! But I'm taking it back to the estate. Terrance' mother is not here? Oh dear. Just Terrance." Her voice rose in hope. "But that *could* be good… it is good to avoid a scene. Oh… oh…" and then it faded in a whimper, and her lip quivered.

Miriam shook her head. This was not good… she was so distressed.

Suddenly Polly had the most beautiful face Bridget could imagine. She saw every line, every crease forged in the fire of life. "What happened? Did you escape without a scene?"

"Oh, there was no scene. Terrance took back the rows. He didn't say much. He was too angry. I knew he was angry; so very angry. As I went to go, he said, 'You will regret this Pollyanna Mansfield. You will regret this day.' Oh, how could I regret being free of him? I am happy. All the silk in the world would never be enough to tie me to him. I'm singing all the way home!" A smile played on her lips as she remembered the freedom of that drive; the elation of following through on a good decision! Suddenly – swiftly, her mood darkened. Her voice became morose. "It is a fool's song!" she said.

"But it's not foolish to sing when you're happy. I sing too…"

"I should have known he would not leave it at that. I know him… better than anyone. But I did not think he would. I should have known! I know what he's like…" She repeated it over and over: *I should have known. I know him.*

Miriam was baffled. Was this just the ramblings of a sick and injured mind… or something more? Such a fantastic story was outside anything she could absorb, so she zoomed in on what she could cope with: soup. "Just a little more broth, Mrs Gartery. A little more… It'll make ye strong."

Bridget's romantic, adventurous spirit had sent her into the new world voluntarily seeking her fortune. She even regretted her impulsiveness a million times over, but the decision was hers. She could live with that. But if this was

Mrs Gartery's history, to be sent against one's will – unjustly, when no crime had been committed. She *had* to let Mrs Gartery finish her tale. "What did you know?"

"I know him… but I didn't know… I should've known. I have an invitation to a ball. Mother and Father are away… Terrance is there, but I avoid him. I will not let him spoil this lovely night: dancing and music, and so many nice men are smiling at me. Oh – such a banquet! And there's roast partridge! That's my favourite…" She sighed almost regretfully. "But we have to go… the music has finished. Home… I feel so sleepy and so happy. It starts to rain… we are nearly home. Oh no! No! Horses and soldiers in uniforms are waiting outside our estate, the house. What can they want? They're searching… They hit you so hard Mary-Jane… are you hurt? Oh! They break your tooth… you are my faithful, beautiful nurse, oh Mary-Jane! The rain is getting heavy… the wind is so strong, lighting and thunder…They are calling from the cellar. They say they have found the rows of silk there. They say I stole them! They say I am greedy and vengeful because Terrance broke off our engagement. But there was never any engagement! They won't listen. They are binding my wrists – ouch! It hurts! They are taking me away. Mary-Jane, you are crying so hard. You are more of a mother to me than Mother." A sob broke in her throat and tears fall down her cheeks, tracing unfamiliar territory. The glazed eyes shone feverishly with anguish. "Mary-Jane…"

"The judge is banging his gavel. He won't stop! He reads out the sentence: the cost of the silks means I am condemned to death. I know that is what Terrance wanted –

he designed it... because I refused him. My father has the Mansfield lawyer's appeal. The sentence is commuted to seven years transportation. Now I am the convict. They say only seven years, but I know it is forever. I am forever condemned. It is still exactly as he intended."

"Oh Mrs Gartery... hush now. Hush. Have some more soup." Miriam was truly distressed. She had seen the marks of a convict on the back of this tall, beautiful lady who had salvaged her life from the squalor of the makeshift taverns along the wharf. Mrs Gartery had even shared her meagre resources with them without hesitation. She had done the same for other girls, helping them to rise above the grime of the street and lift their eyes to dream dreams again. Mrs Gartery told them they were above such filth – so often. And Miriam believed her. She believed it because Mrs Gartery said so. One thought kept flying through Miriam's mind: if she would do that for me... anything, anything she needs, I will do for her.

* * *

Percy sat outside the cave. The elders took Burilda's body. Percy averted his eyes respectfully. He knew what was required as he sat before them. Whoever had done this thing, it was his place to right the wrong. Spilt blood cries for blood spilt. How could Percy explain he had given his allegiance to a Greater Elder now – a brother who had died in his place? Did that not make him bonded to Jesus for life?

He had a choice, and it tore at his heart. "It is not my way..." he said simply. He knew there would be no angry outbursts – their self-control was too great. He almost wanted them to entreaty him to reconsider, but he knew that would never be. As they registered his refusal to pursue revenge, their eyes hooded over and looked past him… through him. Then they turned their backs away.

Percy knew what that meant. It meant he no longer existed. He had failed them. He had caused the death of their own. They had adopted and trusted him, and he had betrayed that trust because he would not extract payback for her blood. Burilda and his unborn child were dead. He hadn't packed the gunpowder in the musket or wielded the bludgeon, but that meant nothing. He should have protected her; instead, he had brought death.

He sat outside the cave as the dark velvety night covered his sorrow like a blanket. He felt torn, shredded. Part of his body had just been amputated without anaesthetic. He could hear the wails from her family echo around the mountains. Percy didn't cry or wail. He did not have that right now he was cast out from the tribe. Now he had to find his own grieving. It was a triple bereavement, his wife, his child, *and* his tribe, and he wondered if it might be more than he could bear.

Percy stared unseeing into the night. "God! What am I going to do?" He was not even aware of his prayer, just an awful numb vacuum sucking in his chest. Unwillingly, but with no power to stop them, images of his life with Burilda flowed and ebbed in his mind:

That hazy first awakening when he was drugged with dehydration and pain, to see her white, even teeth, and chocolate eyes hovering above his face.

The shy and bashful smile as she returned his first kiss.

The hours and days she spent patiently showing him the common knowledge of her people.

The circle of elders as he was ushered into the belonging of the tribe.

Burilda's laughter with the children as he made ridiculous linguistic mistakes and said with all seriousness that he enjoyed eating wombat dung!

Their first argument where he didn't see Burilda for days and every aunt and cousin took her side.

The exhilaration of finding out they were going to become a family and the joy of seeing motherhood dawn in her body like a delicate bush flower opening in the morning sun.

Their baby: the ultimate gift of assimilation. As he lingered over the thought of their baby, tears rolled down his face. Pain welled up within and Percy began groaning, as he never could when the lash hit his back. *Oh, for a thousand beatings*, he thought. *A flogging is easier to bear!*

The pre-dawn air chilled and then a dull overcast sky gradually faded into a murky morning. He sat as the agony awakened again in a fiery, angry grief. The noonday sun moved on under the cover of cloud, oblivious to his ranting. Then it receded into evening once more. Darkness was a relief. He didn't have to look on the world that constantly stabbed him with reminders of what might have been. *My swan, my beautiful black swan*, he cried.

As dawn came again something niggled in his mind… something was pulling him out of the cavernous grief that was threatening to swallow him completely. Something... but he wasn't sure. Was it something Burilda said, something important? He struggled in his mind to see through the fog, but nothing seemed clear.

He decided it was too hard. He surrendered to his grief once more, the awful picture of Burilda's tortured body by the gunya, and the scooped-out bark Coolamon lying beside her, taunting him. He saw that horrific scene again and again. He read the signs of what happened like turning a page in a novel. But this time the bark container and the spilt berries and leaves came sharply into focus. He stared at them in his mind's eye. Why were the medicine-berries so important? Why would she bother picking those berries when they couldn't eat them? Why did she go to so much trouble when they were difficult to find?

It was a puzzle that didn't make sense. His eye was healed. But it would not leave him alone. It niggled at his grief-numbed emotions. If she hadn't tired herself gathering, she could have been back at camp, out of harms' way. Medicine... to make a poultice. Was there another sore eye? Somewhere...

Slowly he remembered: Polly's daughter – Jane, Andi, and Jo... alone at their new bush camp. He remembered everything hazily, like recalling the details of a dream. But he stirred himself to go back to them. He made his way to a water hole. He washed and had a drink. He found some sweet honey-ants, sucking their nectar for energy. For three days he had not eaten.

Gradually he made his way along the creek to their camp. He wasn't exactly sure why it was so important he go to them. All he knew was that they were waiting for him. He did not want more bloodguilt on his hands. That alone was a purpose... no more bloodguilt.

* * *

They sat around the fire eating fish. Percy had speared a good sized yellow-belly in one of the creek's deeper waterholes. Jane cooked it wrapped in some wet paper-bark, like he had shown her when he bought fish to their home. It tasted good, but it was a sad meal. He briefly told them Burilda had died. He even used the word 'murder'. The anger and anxiety that the girls flung out at him, for deserting them, was gone. Grief gave way to sadness that hovered and lingered around them. They said nothing. What words could articulate what they were feeling anyway?

Andi was appalled. She knew the historical stories. She even did an assignment on it once. But this was so different. This was real. She sat for a long time, silently angry at the distant, unemotional accounts of her history textbooks. It was like perjury; a deliberate false representation of what really happened! She hated it, and she wanted it *not* to have happened. But if it really had happened; then telling the truth about it, in all its ugliness, may challenge the world not to minimise this evil, nor repeat it again. It became a seed that nestled in her heart, not out of bitterness, but of deliberation.

Percy roused himself to hunt every morning, but his concentration was dulled. They shared his small offerings gratefully and sometimes he showed them some basic bush-skills that he thought would prove useful. He no longer worried about the tribal laws. Fire-sticks were the domain of men, but if he wasn't around, they needed to know what to do. Life became a tenuous game of survival. He wanted them to have the upper hand against this harsh unforgiving land.

One evening he sat quietly poking the fire with a long stick. "I'm thinking that the fleet will be getting ready to go. I'll be going back to check on your mother tomorrow," he told Jane. Tangibly the mood of the girls lifted. The waiting was over. Life could resume… soon, very soon.

* * *

Percy stood looking at the house through the cover of the scrub. Nothing hung on the clothesline. Everything felt wrong. After the prompting in his spirit on his way to find Burilda, he no longer had the courage to ignore these obscure, undefined feelings. He withdrew back into the bush and went to check the stash of rum Polly had access to.

Rum was something he swore off. He'd seen respectable men lie under the bondage of it. He'd been in bondage. He wasn't about to trade one form of slavery for another. Still, many people persisted in paying for his pelts in rum. His stash became a personal depository, a currency of barter that was well enough accepted for the few things he had need of.

He was surprised the rum was not all gone, but it confirmed to him that not everything had gone as planned. James Gartery would have been able to drink that stash twice over if he'd been given the chance. Percy grabbed two bottles and made his way down to the wharf. The fleet had not gone.

He shuddered at the great hulks that stood motionless in the harbour. Their dark forms carried human cargo. That voyage would never be forgotten. He caught the eye of a stall holder who looked hungrily at his stone bottles. "I be looking to buy some decent clothes," he said. The tall gangly man sized him up and pulled out some britches and a shirt. Percy was unimpressed. "I want a decent set too, with new boots and some extra laces as well. And a hat…" he added.

The man laughed. Percy's direct speech didn't match the raggedy clothes he had on. "How long you been lost? Look like ya bin wandering around in the scrub for years."

"Yeah, something like that…" said Percy with a surly grimace. He had no inclination for banter. He needed information and clung tightly onto his bottles. "Hey, I bin wonderin'… a mate of mine, James Gartery… mariner. He don't seem to be home, but the fleet isn't gone. Know where he is?"

"Gartery? Nah – haven't seen him since he brought his woman down here. Took a load off some rich mongrel for her. A few blokes went with him looking for his kid. Never found her though. Blacks got her…"

Percy lunged forward and grabbed the man by his neck. "You be thinkin' real hard about what happened next!" he said in icy anger. That he could lay guilt on his innocent Burilda so carelessly, sent sparks of rage shooting through him.

The man gasped in shock. His eyes bulged in fear as he looked at the intensity in Percy's face. "Ahhh…. he must 'ave known they'd be coming for his hide," he said, "because I heard he skipped out on *The Helena*" - a merchant rig, goin' back on a Jamaican run. I wouldn't advertise you're his mate though. There's a lota anxious folks lookin' for him."

Percy released him in disgust, and he staggered away rubbing his neck. *"The Helena?* When did she go?"

"Last week sometime…" He sniggered unsympathetically. "He owed you as well – didn't he?" he said knowingly. "You and the rest of the colony! Well, ye won't hear from him again. He's gone… poof!" And he clicked his fingers to emphasise.

If Percy wasn't going to wreak revenge as a tribesman, he would not be extracting payment for this debt in a lesser way as a colonial. He hated that was what he was now. A colonial. He could hear Grandma Hetty say, *"Vengeance is mine sayeth the Lord."* That was so inadequate and did nothing to sooth the anger that burnt holes in his chest. As far as he could see, the barbaric murderer got off scott-free.

Every emotion was raw, frayed at the edges with exposed nerves. Percy intentionally measured his words. "One more thing… where is Mrs Gartery now?'"

"Dunno." The man stretched his rubbery neck. The questions were going on too long.

"Get me the boots then and I'll be going." Percy deliberately sat the stone bottles on an upturned wooden crate, hanging onto the little round handles, to encourage him.

"Boots… ahh! Your lucky stars are shining. Had a pair come in just yesterday. Be your size for sure. I even got one of these…" and he tossed a soft black leather eye patch on the pile.

Percy didn't cringe knowing that all this stuff was retrieved off a cadaver before it was buried. He needed clothes and boots…and he was lucky it was available. Many walked bare-foot, because there was not enough boot-leather to go around. At least it created demand for his pelts.

He verified the story about *The Helena*. Made some further inquiries with skippers and shipmates. The rubberneck was right. James Gartery had vaporised. Equally, so had Polly. No one knew where she was.

He made his way back to Polly's house and knocked. He fully expected the barrel of a musket to poke out the door in answer. Houses that were occupiable did not stay vacant for long. Silence. He went around the back and pushed open the door. There were broken chairs and rats crawling around scavenging for fragments of long-gone scraps. He looked about… reading this scene like he would read the bush. He went out to the fireplace.

He knelt down and poked in the ashes. He picked up a ball of paper charred around the edges. He smoothed it out, black smearing over the letters at the top. It looked official, but the words meant nothing to him. He never bothered to learn to read. Grandma Hetty tried to get him to learn his letters when she gave lessons to the little ones. But it was frustrating, and he was impatient, and he didn't see the point. He wasn't going to read Grandma Hetty's Bible, which is all she read anyway. He nearly tossed the paper back into the ashes, when a faint memory prodded him to take it inside. He shoved it in the makeshift security box that he found overturned on the floor and replaced it in the wall. He tidied up some. He would bring the girls back tonight. His thoughts struggled to see through the haze of his grief to make the girls' home safe for them again. He forgot the paper existed.

* * *

Eliza Thornton sighed despairingly. No one else had the bad luck she was afflicted with. Finally, everything had been going fine, except now Miriam was set on leaving and taking Bridget with her. Bridget was hopelessly scatterbrained so she wouldn't miss her, but Miriam was capable. It didn't matter she wasn't pretty. Pretty girls only attract trouble. If that was the case, Miriam was a safe asset. Eliza was trying to work out how she could make Miriam stay. If begging was required, her pride was not below it. "Miriam dear, you must reconsider! I know you need this position. You won't survive out there. You need me!"

Miriam's face did not change. She had nothing against Mrs Thornton, but she was very much mistaken. She *would* survive. And while Mrs Gartery needed her, Bridget was right – no more could be said. "I'll come back for a few hours each morning Ma'am, while Bridget watches Mrs Gartery. I would not like to see ye stranded."

"Very well – you can stay on for those few hours." Eliza cringed. She hated begging. She sincerely believed her stilted efforts equated with the lowest form of grovelling. But desperate situations called for desperate measures.

"You wouldn't ignite a candle with the warmth of your heart", thought Miriam, as she pursed her lips. "We'll be requiring you to pay us on Saturdays. Bridget can come back to do your

evening chores if you need the extra help," she said in her no-nonsense way.

"Bridget? She barely knows how to turn down a bed!"

"The next fleet will have more to choose from," suggested Miriam quickly. "We'll both be leaving today, Ma'am. Mrs Gartery may get better sooner being in her own home."

"You can't just go!" How ridiculous and unreasonable she was being for a commoner. "It's not like Mrs Gartery deserves anything. She owes us! She was a wreck beyond help when she got here, and we have nursed and looked after her! The Doctor was most emphatic about how kind we were."

"The doctor said she needs lots of rest and familiar surroundin's. That's why we're going. I'll come back in the morning and help you Ma'am. And since your charity cost you so – you can take what is owed from my allowance. We'll not be wanting to be in your debt." With that Miriam stood up and gathered her bag of things, and together with Bridget she guided Mrs Gartery out the door and down the path.

* * *

It was dark as Percy and the girls made their way over the clearing to the house. Suddenly he stopped. "Shush! There's someone in there." He sent them back under the cover of trees. He glanced through the cracks of the shuttered windows into the yellowed glow inside. He could hear muffled talking. He bumped a pile of shattered chairs he had stacked against the wall that afternoon. He swore under his breath as they crashed. He would never have made such a mistake once.

Immediately the talking stopped. The weak light inside was snuffed out. Great. He didn't want a scene... but he felt protective of this house on behalf of Jane. It was *her* home. No one else had rights to it. Fancy someone taking up residency in the few hours since he left. "Oh God – why has this gotta be complicated? I've just about had all the complicated I can take. Just keep it simple until I find Polly and those girls' folks. Then I can be me on my way. But I said I would find 'em, and I want to be a man of me word. Grandma Hetty used to say you wouldn't tempt a man beyond what he could bear. Please... don't start with me!"

He picked up the leg of a stool that lay on the ground, and silently opened the door. In the dimness he could make out a shadow of a form that slid up to shut the door as carelessly as if it had blown open by the wind. By instinct he grabbed, turned the body around in one movement and locked his captive with the wooden shaft against their neck as if it was a headstock.

There was a terrified squeal, and his hostage started to kick and scream like a stuck pig. A woman. Great. He shoved his hand over her mouth and muffled the sound. Someone fumbled with a candle. As the flame of the candle took and spun weird shadows around the room, he saw a young woman facing him, her face shrouded in shadows. What got his attention was the barrel of a musket pointing at his head. Her voice was like ice. "Put the stick down real quiet like and back out the door. You don't belong here, and you ain't invited.

His grip tightened. "That's where you're mistaken Ma'am. I have every right to be here, and just 'cause you

115

moved in – that don't make it your place. Now put your loaded rod down." He shifted his stock-hold, threatening to tighten it around her neck. His captive stopped thrashing and started whimpering uncontrollably. The loaded musket didn't shift. She shoved it forward again. Evidently, she wasn't going to back down.

His sight adjusted to the dark. She could only identify women. Oh terrific. It wasn't going to be "simple" after all – that was evident. He dropped the stick and moved away. She fell to the floor, weak and incoherent. The musket girl edged sideways and threw some rope to another who stood frozen in the corner shadows. "Tie him up."

"Well, then, let me explain… I…" A scarf was stuffed into his mouth to gag his objections. He stood quietly. He watched them through his unpatched eye. They were barely women… young but experienced in self-preservation. Still, he wasn't about to fight girls. He'd change his plans. They'd have to go back to the bush-camp. But the person who tied his arms did a good job and he couldn't move.

"Now what are we gunna do?" said the musket-bearer. Something about the statement made him look again. Did he know these squatters? The girl, who tied his arm, picked up the woman at his feet.

"Oh ma'am. Look at ye. Come and sit over here," she coaxed. The one holding the musket sounded ticked off. "You just undid a whole lot of good," she accused him. "She was the best she been in weeks and now ya undid that in one foul swoop. You terrified her… you held her by her neck…

how could ye?" Percy could not respond. The scarf was tightly shoved in.

He looked at the shadow of the woman sitting limply on a small straight-backed chair. A familiar stab leapt inside him as he recognised that silhouette... but as he looked again there was nothing familiar about the cowering form. If only he could find Polly: Tall, capable, sensible Polly. She would be so distressed over her daughter. Polly had sent Jane to him in trust, and he had no intention of betraying such confidence. Polly had been his only neighbour in this foreign place. Burilda had been family, but Polly was his neighbour. It was funny how Grandma Hetty seemed more alive now, than when he had been living under her matriarchal wing. She would have said, "Love ye neighbour as yourself..."

* * *

"Typical," said Jo as they sat in the cover of the shadows made by the faint moonlight. The silence was long and protracted. "He's going to disappear again. I knew it."

"How? We saw him go over there and he hasn't come back..." Andi was trying hard not to let the panic rise again. She pushed it down. Percy had always been so thoroughly straight with them, even when he had no need to be.

"We can't see a thing Andi. He could've gone around the other side and given us the slip. Since he brought us back, he probably thinks that this is as much obligation he owes us."

"But he promised...." That quiver came from Jane.

"Promised what?" Jo *had* played along. But just now, as she sat in inky shadows looking at the gloomy outline of the dark drab hut, she confessed to herself and to the others, she had been seriously duped. "He never promised anything."

"No – you are wrong. He'll keep his word. I'm sure…" But even as she said it, Andi wasn't so sure.

"Get real Andi. He's given out on us."

Andi reluctantly admitted that Jo was probably right. Not that she could blame him. Had anything ever gone well for Percy? "Well, what do we do now?"

Jo had told the Green Team girls over and over: *We stick together.* But here, it didn't seem like anyone else thought that was important at all. It is one thing realising you are on your own. It is another to know what to do next. "Maybe we should find out who Percy heard in the house." They believed Percy's report that Jane's father had left on the fleet and her mother was away. Percy never said where she was staying; only that she'd be back soon. That meant that if someone else was inside, they had taken unrightful vacant possession.

Jo took the lead and the girls followed quietly behind her. As they pressed against the mud walls and listened intently. They could hear someone whimpering and the gentle voice of another trying to soothe. Quietly Jo peeked through the gaps in the shuttered windows. Her eyes, adjusting to the muted candlelight, widened in surprise as she saw Percy bound and gagged in the dimly lit corner. She saw the frame of a woman with a musket. Whoever was making the sounds were out of sight. She slid down onto her haunches, her pupils widely dilated from the dark and shock. Percy was being held hostage. Andi was right. He had tried.

Jo listened for a while, trying to do a mental count of who was where. They slid around the back to the garden. They quickly formulated a desperate, impulsive plan, distributing the few garden tools they could find. Then she signalled for them to follow.

They crept in silently and undetected, then burst into the sitting room. Andi jabbed a shovel handle into the musket bearer's back. "Drop it, now!" she growled, jabbing her ribs, seriously calling on her acting experience as a school musical gangster. The musket was dropped like a red-hot branding iron. It hit the floor and exploded into the wall shooting powdery mud over the room. The dust settled, and Percy struggled to his feet. Jo pulled the scarf from his mouth.

"Ye ain't supposed to be here! Ye mothers would never forgive me if ye hurt."

Jo chuckled. "Well, you're not doin' real well by yourself…"

Every eye turned towards her as she spoke. "Jo?"

"Yeah?" she slowly responded, suspiciously.

All of a sudden, everyone was talking at once.

"It's you?"

"Jo – Andi?"

"Mims?"

"It's really you!"

"Bridget!"

"Who'se he?"

"Mama?" Jane was looking at the crumpled form on the floor. It quietened at the sound of her voice. "Mama!"

"Polly? Oh my!" Percy bolted to the heap and lifted her up as she lashed out defensively.

Her strong arms and legs violently struck at him. "Off me! Get him off me!" she screeched. Percy sat her on their one remaining chair and backed away as Bridget threw herself in between them. She flung her fists in the air, her arms spinning like a child's novelty windmill.

Percy calmly held Bridget at arms' length. "Go away!" she yelled, "You horrible man! Leave her alone!"

Percy looked at the dark ceiling, wondering why it seemed to be falling in on him. *'God, I'm trying here, but it ain't workin'. You'd better help out, or I'll quit. I know I will…'* He threw the ultimatum at God as if he expected it would hold water.

Bridget continued shouting, tears streaming down her face as she gradually stopped her floundering. "Go away! If Percy was here, he'd sort you out!"

He shook his head as if something had flown in his ear. "Who?" His shocked question pacified her momentarily.

"Percy. Our friend. He'd fix ya!"

He looked at her for a moment until he registered. "Oh!" He dropped her arms and burst out laughing out of pure relief that echoed into the night. The sudden release of deep tension over this absurd confusion sent waves of healing through him.

Andi stood beside Jane as she stroked her mother's hair, smiling at their secret of Percy's transformation. "Oh Mama, Mama. Sweet Mama. We're home now. We're home now," Jane whispered.

Bridget stood there stunned as she watched this mysterious good-looking stranger shaking his head as he laughed. "That's not funny, he really would!" He sort of looked familiar, but then, any face Bridget looked at for a while became her best friend.

Miriam watched him closely also – the humour of the situation seriously evading her. He flung back his head, his patch slipped down and suddenly Miriam realised that this man, with his continental haircut, respectable clothes and leather eye patch was their very own Percy. "Percy?" She was annoyed her bravery had been wasted on harmless Percy. The look of revelation which wiped across her face, sent Andi into fits of giggles. Jo joined in the contagious release of mirth. How about that? Andi was a fantastic hairdresser! But more importantly, they had stuck together after all.

* * *

9.

Life settled into a routine of chores. Percy built a lean-to onto the back of the hut so that he could stay close by. He began the process of rebuilding his life. He re-established his trapping rounds and developed a trade in furs and pelts. He watched for an opportunity to move out of trapping into other lines of work. He observed with interest the increasing fascination with sheep farming in the colony and disregarded it as an option when he saw the damage that the large numbers of cloven hooves did to the landscape of his beloved Burilda's homeland. No, it was more than that. It was his homeland now.

Miriam capably took over the management of the house. She went to Mrs Thornton's every morning at half past four and returned to do her allotted chores at home. Percy made Polly a chair... deep and comfortable, with arm rests that the girls helped him pad and cover with soft leather. She loved her armchair, but instinctively distanced herself from *'that man'* who had held her in a headlock that first night they came home.

Jo worked on their garden with renewed industry. The girls went to the government stables for manure to improve the quality of their soil. They were able to acquire three pullets, a cockerel, and an ewe sheep. These investments were Miriam's idea. The chooks were a delight to Jo who had them perching on her shoulder when she worked in the garden. The first tiny immature egg caused excitement out of all proportion to the size of the offering. The ewe was an old thing that had just about given out on its lambing days, Miriam sheered the fleece. They combined the wool with fur taken off Percy's hides and spun them together to make blankets. One morning they came out to find the ewe had given birth to a lamb. It took Andi and Jo a while to get used to the idea, but Bridget milked the ewe every morning, for fresh milk. Any water from the weekly baths or washing went onto their garden. Gradually they began to see the rewards for their labours, as green healthy seedlings began to emerge.

One day Andi was looking at a small prayer book she found in Polly's room as she was cleaning, when Jane came in. "Oh no - don't! Mama never liked people touching that book."

"Does she read it?"

"She used to... a lot. But not now." Jane's little face was sad.

"Perhaps you could read it to her?"

"I can't read. She was going to teach me letters. Mims and Bridget can't read neither..."

"But I can... and so can Jo!" said Andi excitedly. Suddenly she saw a unique opportunity. "And I could teach you, so you can read! Oh Janie, your Mum would love it if you could read to her – don't you think?"

"You reckon? Could I?" Her eyes lit up with the unimaginable! To read!

They both went out to the sitting room where Polly sat on her chair by the open shuttered window, restlessly picking at her skirt. "Mama, Andi would like to read to you... from your little book. Would you like that?" Polly looked with interest at the little bright face before her. It was so beautiful, so delicate, so clear. She shrugged at the words she was saying. They swirled in a fuzzy audible haze that she couldn't really understand. But it didn't matter, not so long as the face stayed.

Andi opened the book and sat near the window beside her. She started reading, slowly, stumbling over the unfamiliar old English phrases. Polly stroked Jane's face as the rhythm of the words soothed and calmed. When Andi closed the book, Polly looked at her. "Thank you," she said, "That was nice." So reading was added into their daily routine. Jane would brush her mother's hair or file her nails or massage her feet as Andi read prayers and scripture from the book. And when they had finished the book, they started again, and then again. Andi showing her words, and letters as she did.

When Andi told Jo of her plan to start teaching Jane actual English lessons, Jo laughed outright. "You can't be serious. You're not a teacher!"

"It's not so silly. She can't read... and she wants to. There isn't a school. If we don't... who will?"

Jo knew where this was going. "But we haven't even finished school ourselves! How can we pretend to be teachers?"

"We'll just be showing them what we know... like sharing stuff. Even if we get them to read as well as your brother in grade three, it will be much more than they know now. How can that be wrong?"

"It'll be wrong if we do it wrong. We know nothing about teaching. People go to university for that."

"Not here they don't," said Andi quickly.

"Fair point…" Jo conceded. "But why not include Mims and Bridget as well?"

Andi spoke to them and was overwhelmed by their enthusiasm. But was baffled how they could teach the alphabet without pencils and paper. When Percy returned from his trapping trip, Andi spoke to him about her plans to teach the girls to read. Miriam knew literacy gave people an edge. She had long suspected Mrs Thornton took liberties. Mims believed she had paid off the debt of Mrs Gartery's care long ago, but she could not actually prove or account for it. The unfortunate reality was that she could never afford a tutor. It seemed this remarkable opportunity had just fallen from heaven itself. Bridget's motivation was more about reading about pretty things she could buy from the wharf markets.

Percy looked sceptical. "Ye wanta teach 'em to read?"

"Yeah… and write… numbers." Andi sighed. She knew she could do it! "Why not? They really want to learn…"

"No reason. I guess…" He seemed dubious.

"Reading is important. I think Jane just wants to read to her Mum at the moment – but it will help her in lots of things later on."

"Like…"

"Well, she can read stories, and journals and letters and…." Andi tried to think of what would appeal to the mind of a man. "… contracts. Think of the influence she could have, being able to read for herself and not take someone else's word for it."

Percy jolted. *Influence?* "Well, there you go. My point. Women don't do business."

"Sure, they do. They buy stuff… and work…that's business. They shouldn't be taken advantage of, just because they have to trust people are being straight when they're not." Andi was surprised Percy would demean their right to learn. It was not something she expected from him.

"Well, I do business," said Percy quietly.

Suddenly Andi twigged. "Well, you could check out what we're doing. Just to make sure it is okay. If you sat in on the lessons – it would give you a better idea of what we might need."

He nodded seriously. "Maybe… What would you be needing to do this?"

"Well, I'm not sure, but at our school we had desks and chairs… a whiteboard, and then we had books and pens… so we could practise."

"Whiteboard?"

"Up front, so the teacher can show us stuff – like this…" and she drew a sketch in the dirt. He left then and returned with large sheets of bark, stripped from trees that they flattened and cut to make practice boards. They washed down the side wall of the hut to use to write up lessons; charcoal was their writing implement; they moved logs into place to sit on. They washed it all off at the end of each lesson.

So, they started. The eager students, even with limited resources made great progress, taking turns to read from Polly's prayer book as their only textbook.

Soon Miriam and Percy started coming home with things to add to their collection – Percy got hold of a Bible, Miriam scrounged discarded gazettes, letters, governor's notices and briefs. They read and devoured anything they could lay their hands on.

* * *

Percy went away for extended times on his rounds. He had to go on large detours to avoid crossing tribal boundaries. He spent these trips deep in thought. He made no conscious effort to pray, but his heart naturally wanted to talk with God as his companion. One night as he sat by his campfire, lazily poking the coals with a stick, he thought of the bizarre circumstances he found himself in. He had become the guardian and provider for five young ladies and Polly. He must be the only fellow in the entire colony in such a position. It was quite confused how it all came about.

Polly... dear Polly. She had always done so well. He admired her survival. She never talked to him about her previous life – before being transported to Australia, but he had pieced together enough to know they were from different ends of the social spectrum. If they had ever met on that other shore, they would not have even talked. Once Polly told him she married James Gartery on the ship because she knew one needed to be a wife to be adequately treated in the colony. Single women were used and abused in the penal settlement. That was commonly acknowledged. She had figured marriage to a sailor would afford a fair amount of independence, with the extended periods of absence balancing out the duty required while he was landed. Her marriage was a strategy of self-preservation, but in the end, her attempt to clutch at stability had done the opposite.

Percy poked at the ashes as red coals fell in on themselves. Polly. His heart ached over the layers of trauma imposed on her life. *God! Can I help bring her back? God? Where is she underneath all that pain? She must be in there... waiting to be released! Didn't Grandma Hetty say... (didn't I even read it myself?) that you came to set the captive free, to make the blind, see?* A groan welled up within him for the first time since Burilda's death, not for his own pain, but for the pain of another. *God! I am blind in one eye – but Polly's blindness is darker than mine. Oh God. Jesus, heal her – release her! Bring her back into the light.*

* * *

Polly opened her eyes. "Janie? Janie!" She felt a panic as she sat up on the bed. "Jane! Where are you?"

"Here Mama... I'm here. What can I get for you?" Jane flew into the room. Her mother had called for her – by name! She swept her mother up in a huge hug, tears rolling down her face! "Oh Mama..."

"Oh Janie. Oh, my little darling. You're safe. You're here. Thank God!" Polly pulled her in tight, responding with a hug that she never wanted to escape from. Cleansing tears rolled down her face, washing the terror away.

"Oh Mama... you have been really sick. We've been praying so hard."

"Sweet Jane. I'm getting better... I know it..." She stopped and held her daughter at arm's length, drinking in the sight of her as if she had been in a dry, parched place for a long time. "I had this dream you were reading to me... but I never taught you your letters. Is it true? Were you reading?"

Jane giggled – a tinkle of laughter sprinkled delight around her mother's eyes. "Yes! Oh Mama. I'm not very good... but I am learning. Andi is teaching us. And Jo sometimes... but she's not very patient. Andi is good at explaining things."

"Oh Janie, you seem so grown up. Would you read something? Show me how you can."

Janie quickly retrieved her mother's prayer book. "Mama, I hope you don't mind," she said apologetically as she opened the cover, "but you seemed to enjoy listening to the prayers so much... and it was all we had. We have other stuff to read now. But to start with, there wasn't much."

"Hush child, it's okay. If you read prayers, that is a good thing to learn. Read me one about being free... I'd like that. It's been a long time..."

Jane turned over the pages. *"Hear what comfortable words our Saviour Chriſt saith unto all that truly turn to Him... Come unto me all that travail and are heavy laden and I will refresh you. So, God loved the world, that He gave His only begotten Son, to the end that all that believe in Him ſhould not periſh, but have everlaſting life..."*

"Aye, that is a comfort..."

She sat up straight as Bridget brought in some porridge, served with ewe milk. Bridget stopped in the doorway, her eyes wide, as she saw Polly sitting with Jane who was chatting delightedly with her mother. "Good mornin' Ma'am! Oh, it is so good to see ye this morning. It is a lovely morning outside. Perhaps ye'd like to sit out on the verandah for a time when ye ready?"

"Slowly Bridget… Jane's been telling me she's learning to read. We will not interrupt her lessons. I would like to see them in progress." But even after breakfast, Polly fell asleep exhausted as the lessons commenced.

Gradually, Polly emerged from her shell. She had good days when she tackled old tasks with vigour. And then there were bad days when she sighed and slept and wandered around the house trying to fight her way out from underneath the black blanket that threatened to smother her again. On those days, she particularly liked Jane to read to her. Gradually there were less of these sorts of days to interrupt the flow of their life.

Polly was amazed at what capable young women her girls had become. Miriam's work afforded a small income to supplement Jo's garden. It was a source of delight as each new treasure was picked and brought to the table. She was able to get a variety of garden seed from the Governor's store and even invested in a fig tree and pear tree, which they tended with obsessive protectiveness.

The lessons progressed under Andi's tutelage. The girls' skills in number and reading progressed; writing being the most difficult challenge as they lacked the materials needed to become competent scribes. It was an exciting day when Percy arrived with ink and quills and a quantity of low-quality paper. The development of their literacy increased exponentially.

* * *

Percy's progress lagged behind the others. His trips away meant he had to wait for long periods before he could get his questions answered. He took his Bible and read out

130

loud by the firelight, frustrated by the huge gaps in his understanding. But patience had been unwillingly carved into his character and he persevered with the staying power of a leech.

Polly acknowledged the inclusion of Percy in Andi's class with cool distance. She recognized the value of Percy's presence in this colonial world where a man's influence outstripped any female voice – regardless of intelligence or virtue. Besides, he had provided sanctuary for Jane when she needed it. It wasn't that she didn't trust Percy. She did – unaccountably without reservation, but the friendship they used to have, was a vague memory that didn't seem real. He continued to bring food with regular reliability, and she took it with formal words of remote gratitude.

Percy had no heart to confront her coldness. Perhaps it was an outcome of her trauma. He battled with himself, over what he should do. He could not bring himself to charge money for the supplies as he used to… because he knew there were no means for her to pay. To charge less than their worth would be an affront to her pride. But not to be involved in their lives at all, and risk that poverty would rise up and strangle them again, was equally impossible.

In the end he opted to sustain the status quo, with that same air of formality. He approached Polly one morning as he readied his traps and swag to leave. He chose the most reserved and official terms he could think of. "Mrs Gartery, I'll be going this morning. I am wondering now that you are well and established, that I need to be looking for a place to base myself when I come into the settlement to do my trading.

I am looking to pay for the room out the back, in exchange for the supplies I bring ye – if ye still be wanting them - of course." He looked away. He realised his averted eyes was not recognised as the respectful diffidence taught in his Aboriginal training. He just couldn't look at her. Why was that? What was it that got under his skin?

Polly regarded him coolly. He had changed, and those changes unsettled her. She wished things could revert to how they were. And if not, she wished he would go away and never come back. But on the long weeks when he was away, sometimes she found herself looking out past the trees that were gradually being cleared away for more houses to be built, to see if his hat was walking down the track with the spoils of his expedition slung over his shoulder.

Somehow his trips just became longer and more extended in between the times when he would return. Those trips were to satisfy himself that all was well with 'his' girls. While he was away, their faces would haunt him. Little Jane with her long strawberry-blond hair bouncing out to tell him of some exciting new discovery, chatting with an exuberance that entangled her in his heart.

Miriam began to share dreams and ambitions that wanted to soar above any of her previous expectations. It had to do with teaching girls herself, spurred on by the example of Mrs Gartery's compassion and Andi's low-cost education.

Even Bridget confided in Percy, confessing her enamoured interest in the young cousin of Mrs Thornton's sister-in-law, who was increasingly outspoken against his aunt's "Bunyip aristocracy". It was what he called her fake attempts to create colonial nobility in a society that had always snubbed its nose at authority.

Andi and Jo? He no more understood those two than when he had first stumbled across them after the storm. He was still unable to find any trace of the camping party that they had been separated from. They seemed happy enough with what was at hand.

No, it was just Polly who unsettled him. He didn't know why she should. It was best just to stay out of the way... for as long as he could.

* * *

Percy stood outside the Colonial Secretaries office with his 'new' third-hand coat firmly buttoned and his boots smartly polished. He had in his hand some letters and waited for this interview nervously. He had made inquiries how to extend his trading routes and diversify into other colonial markets to supplement his furs. He was submitting applications to the governor for land.

"His Excellency is extremely busy; make it brief," said the man curtly as he stiffly shuffled a wad of papers in his hand and opened the door. He stood well back and cringed as he walked past. Percy entered the office and stood, uncertain as to what the right thing would be to do. He looked around at the austere furnishings that were transplanted from an overseas empire. He saw the Governor standing by the window deep in reflection, holding a letter in his hand. Percy tentatively cleared his throat, and the Governor looked up surprised.

"Oh, I'm sorry." He apologetically waved the letter in his hand, his eyes clouded with responsibility. "It seems every correspondence brings bad news. The saying *'no news is good news'* applies to colonial life at all times, it seems."

Percy hardly knew how to respond. The man was the Governor, an official representative of the King. It didn't seem reasonable he would have a personal life – or feelings. But in that moment of vulnerability, Percy saw a man like himself – with fears and dreams and aspirations and affections. "I'm sorry to hear it sir. Is it news of your family at home?"

He looked up, startled again from his reverie. "I'm sorry. Mr Percival Holmes, is that right? Yes, take a seat." He indicated the leather chair by his desk. "No, no – this is nothing of a personal nature – although as Governor I think every matter takes on a personal tone. It is news of a merchant ship on a run to Jamaica – the Master who skippered her was a friend of mine. She was lost going around the Horn. The man survived typhoons and scurvy; every affliction of the sea imaginable. He'd had spent some time with my wife and I when he was here some months hitherto. Such a short time ago… but it seems like a lifetime. Quite literally, it seems."

"Jamaica?" There was something in Percy's voice that made the man look up from his desk again. *"The Helena?"*

"Yes. You knew her?

"I knew one of the crew. The husband of …"

"Aye… It is a hard thing – losing a friend."

Percy sighed, almost regretfully. "He may not have even been on board…"

"I have a list… these others are just names on a sheet of paper to me… to someone they are family or friend. If ye be wanting to have a look at it, ye are welcome." He handed the sheet to Percy. He didn't even ask if he could read. It was assumed of course. He had with him letters of application.

Percy took the sheet and looked laboriously down the names. The ledger was handwritten, scratchy and difficult to decipher. He shook his head. "I am thinking it is too much of a shock to take in. Could I have a copy to take to the man's wife? He'd be Gartery, James Gartery." He returned the sheet.

The man looked down the list of names – somehow a mutual tragedy, bound these two extremes momentarily together… the ruler and the ex-convicted. "Ecclestone, Forbes, Gartery… James. Yes. Crew. I'm sorry. I'll get my secretary to write a letter of notification to his wife. If you wait after our business and give him the details, we can make certain that it is delivered as promptly as possible." He set aside the letter, almost regretfully, and turned to the business at hand. "Now about these applications…" and he shifted into administration gear and went through the things he needed clarified.

* * *

10.

Polly woke up one Sunday with the desire to celebrate the restoration of their life together. At breakfast she announced, "It such a beautiful day, I think we will take a picnic to the beach." Jane greeted the prospect of the outing with exclaims of delight!

Jo and Andi looked at each other amazed. Was this really the same woman who tackled every task so aggressively when they first arrived? Sure, they understood she was recovering, but they fully expected that as she got better, she would resume her iron-fisted reign. Perhaps their prayers *had* poured an oil of healing over her which had seeped into those obscure scarred and calloused places. They shook their head amazed. The change had been so gentle, so subtle, that if Polly had not announced the extraordinarily frivolous notion of celebrating with a *picnic*, they could have missed it completely.

The excitement of packing up their picnic filled the house. Even Miriam, with her serious perspective on everything, smiled and grabbed a book that she had begged from Mrs Thornton's limited library. "It will be the perfect opportunity to read," she said enthusiastically. They donned their hats with great aplomb. Walking with gusto they set out, their skirts billowing over the native coarse grasses, like fleet ships in the harbour setting sail on their voyage to The Cape.

Polly knew exactly where to have their picnic. There was a little cove, private and out of the way, where glorious yellow-gold sand bunched in dunes between dark ancient rocks. They set up their picnic in the shade of the rocks, soaking in the fresh salt air, and the listening to hovering seagulls that squawked over the rocks and the gentle wash of waves on the sand.

Their picnic was simple fare, but to this party on the beach, it was like a banquet. They had a round of pan-fried scones; sun dried tomato pieces from Jo's garden; and dehydrated, salted SUPERB (an acronym that stood for: "**s**omething **u**ndefined **P**ercy **e**ats, **r**ecommends, or **b**rings"). This last menu item was named when Percy had brought some meat with him that he was unwilling to name. Andi had tried to explain the idea of Acronyms in one of her lessons and had used it as a silly illustration. The thing stuck. Everything Percy brought since – whether animal or vegetable, was now designated SUPERB. The fact that his 'superb' food was unspecified, as far as Andi was concerned – was often helpful!

After lunch, Mims and Andi sat on the rug totally absorbed in discussing words, grammar, and books. Jo produced a ball from her bag. She had made it out of an old stocking stuffed tight with rag-wadding, that been stitched and turned in on itself and restitched, again and again, creating a missile the size of a tennis ball. Jo was proud of her efforts, and she helped Jane scour the beach for the right piece of driftwood to serve as a bat. Jane was intrigued. Her short life had not included many children as play mates, and she was excited by Jo's promise to teach her a new game: beach-cricket.

Bridget joined in with enthusiasm. The pitch was the hard wet sand of the receding tide. The stumps were made of driftwood propped up against some rocks. Bridget bowled as Jo guided Jane's bat to hit the ball. Bridget was natural athlete and soon had the idea. Jane on the other hand, found the concept totally baffling. In the end she decided that bowling suited her best. The fun that ensued had everyone in stitches. Bridget set out chasing the ball backwards and forwards, tripping over her long skirt and diving in vain attempts to catch Jo out. In the end it was Jane who bowled her cleanly!

Polly looked at the girls playing this version of the gentleman's game she knew from home. Once she would have thought it was impudent. Now Polly was looking through the lens of a woman who nearly lost everything. She gratefully acknowledged God had restored her ability to enjoy this fragile life.

She felt her heart warm and swell towards Andi and Jo who had shown friendship to her daughter, and those in her care. All the evidence was that these two girls came from some upper-class English family… just like herself… but with a difference. They came without the prejudice that rocked her family's glasshouse of respectability. The Mansfield family despised felons, so how do you respond when one of your own becomes a convicted criminal? The stones they had thrown at others came hurtling back to shatter the traditional fragile walls that held her family together.

But it wasn't only her family who threw stones. It was those like them. Yet Andi and Jo had never despised Jane for being a colony-born currency-kid… or Bridget for being scatter-brained and distractible, or Miriam for being plain and humourless, or herself for being weak and broken. Polly knew that these were the things that lacked the polish she once so stringently adhered to. She struggled for such perfection because somehow, if she attained it, she believed she would find a place in this new world. Yet now she recognised that this new world was just like the old world, and it didn't want to allocate places to the uncomfortable people who disrupted their streamline studio oil-portraits of tradition.

The funny thing was she didn't even want to become part of that shallow side of society... not at all! She just wanted a place that could be her own. She wanted to believe that would give meaning to her pointlessly sabotaged life. She once thought by helping stranded girls she would take the power to define that meaning... and it had worked for a while. Yet even that had proven to be just a fragile passing privilege and not a solid rock on which to build her identity. Yes, it was the foundation that she needed. That underpinning solid comfort. Then she realised that in those gentle words, spoken and reread, the message had got through...in the most wonderful ways. She smiled as she realised her foundation-rock already had a Name!

She opened her prayer book and it fell open to page 270. An Evening Prayer: Psalm 98. *"O sing unto the Lord a new fong: for he hath done marvellous things... Shew yourfelves joyful unto the Lord, all ye lands: fing, rejoice and give thanks. Praife the Lord upon the harp: fing to the harp, with a pfalm of thankfgiving... Let the fea make a noife, and all that therein is. Let the floods clap their hands, and let the hills be joyful together before the Lord: for he is come to judge the earth. With righteoufnefs fhall he judge the world: and the people with equity."*

It was not strange to her that many of the "s" letters were replaced by "f". It was familiar to her. Polly smiled to herself. Is this what the waves of the sea were singing about today? A righteous God who arbitrates with equity! She had seen plenty of judges who didn't. Her eyes sparkled as she watched Jane bowl another ball to Bridget who lifted the makeshift bat high and whacked it hard. Jo's determination to end Bridget's beginners-luck innings was competitively fierce. She ran backwards, arms outstretched, skirts flapping as she reached up to catch the ball that was momentarily suspended in the air. She continued running, her eyes fixed on the ball, splashing in the water that quickly became deeper. She made one last dive, up and backwards, landing as foaming waves rolled in and dunked her completely. Jo came up spluttering, her trophy held high. "Out! I've caught you! You're out! Yes!" She splashed and danced around in jubilation.

Bridget stood laughing; she may have been caught out, but she made Jo work hard for her wicket. Suddenly Jane screamed: a high-pitched squeal of terror. Polly stumbled to her feet.

"Jo! Out!" called Polly urgently, as she ran towards her, slow motion pumping her body forward, ploughing through a molasses atmosphere thick with fear.

Jo lowered the ball in shock. "But Bridget's out! Fair and square..." She began to protest as she looked at Jane – still screaming and pointing at her. Confusion washed over her like the surf that pummelled against her billowing skirts. The taste of the afternoon, with all its good humour and fellowship, evaporated. Jo wiped the hair out of her eyes as Polly ran towards her, ploughing through the seawater to reach her.

Just as Polly reached her, Jo's feet were knocked out from underneath her. The water rushed through her hair and eyes, the air in her lungs was forced out as something rammed hard against her back. Polly dived forward, clutching at her arms. She grabbed fiercely, dragging desperately against the dark grey shadow that menaced the water unseen behind Jo. Unexpectedly then, Bridget was there with the bat, banging blindly in terror and anger at the creature that would try to snatch her friend. With a final rip, Jo's skirts gave way in the water, and with a flick of its smooth sleek tail, Jo was released into the arms of Polly.

She dragged Jo to the edge of the water, tears of anxiety mixing with the sea salt, stinging her eyes. They collapsed in the sand. They lay there gasping, Jo coughing, gulping large whoops of air, her lungs burning in pain with each breath. Jane came running and tumbled on her mother, sobbing in relief. "Oh Mama! Oh Mama! It was so big…" Andi gently parted the torn edges of her skirts and saw a shallow gouge in Jo's side. Without hesitation Miriam tore her petticoat and applied it to the wound. Jo winced in pain but she was otherwise unharmed.

Jo's gasping slowed. Her frame trembled. "What happened? What was it?"

Polly squeezed her eyes tight, and tears escaped. "A shark… a small one I think…" Jo's blousy skirts created a net of protection against its teeth as it rolled in, to attack. Polly had seen people jump ship to escape their captors only to become victims to these appetites.

They huddled together, breathing out the terror of what might have been and inhaling thanks for protection. Each gasp bound them even more tightly together as a family.

* * *

11.

Andi and Bridget supported Jo's shaken frame as they walked home. The return trip seemed much longer than when they had set out that morning. As they turned the last curve in the track Polly froze. Outside their hut stood a man in colonial red uniform, his horse tethered to the verandah.

Polly looked down the track and another stormy night with military uniforms and horses, loomed close again. History was being repeated in the present. She swayed weakly. Miriam quickly came to her side and held her arm. "Ma'am, it is okay. We just need to find out what he wants. They won't be taking you away. Not again."

Polly looked at this girl, who seemed agelessly wise. She was shocked that Mims knew her secret. *"Oh God,"* her heart screamed. *"I can't do this again. I can't! Be my strength, be my refuge, be our protection. Would Ye save us from being ripped apart from the jaws of a shark, to be torn apart again by sharks of a different kind? Oh God have mercy!"*

Polly took some deep gulping breaths and lifted her chin resolutely. Mims was right of course. *"The Lord shall preserve thy going out, and thy coming in: from this time forth for evermore,"* she whispered half to herself and half to the girls. She shakily stepped out, speaking words of comfort and strength and reliance to herself, over and over.

The young solider stepped forward, his face clouded with the inconvenience of his errand. These people were common; the residence made that clear. The Governor had clearly overstated the responsibility of his mission. "Mrs James

Gartery?" Polly nodded her assent, brushing her tangled sea washed hair from her face. The lad continued abruptly. "His Excellency the Governor, insisted this notice be served to you only in person." He thrust an envelope at her, turned on his heel and remounted. "Good day to you Madam," and he spurred his horse around, so he could return to his colonial post.

Polly sat weakly on the step. Her hands trembled at she broke the seal and unfolded the letter. She read it three times, trying to see past the official lines for the facts. It was plain enough. James was dead. She leaned back weakly on the rough sawn verandah post. Was it true? The letter said he had gone down with a lost merchant ship bound for the Caribbean. It was too confusing. What about James' naval commission? Yet the official insignia at the head of the paper gave credence to its message.

Polly's tears fell, unheeded. Some tears were because she didn't have to hold her breath any longer, waiting for a day when he would return a visitation of horror. Some she shed mourning the loss of her daughter's father, if for no other reason than he gave her life. But most were for the loss of an intention. She never loved him. Polly knew that, and she didn't even regret it. She also knew James despised her, even though it had not started out that way. But somewhere, there had been the intention to be a good wife to her husband, to have companionship and a shared vision, but none of those things ever came to be. They were like faded old flowers that once bloomed, which now stood crisp and brown in a jar like a memorial to a forgotten past. She had long given up thinking the flowers could come to life, and as she wept, she washed away the remaining petals of those dreams. How long she sat she didn't know, but when she stood, she somehow felt stronger, more resolute. From this day forward there would be new dreams, new intentions that would go further than well-meaning resolutions.

A group of men travelling up the track caught her eye. She waited for them as they drew near. She did not know them. There was not a familiar face among them. One man stepped forward. McCoster was a burly, hairy fellow with black tuffs of body-hair poking out from under his collar. His thick eyebrows joined across his brow in a mountain ridge. He frowned as he thrust a copy of a circular at her. It described the fate of *The Helena* and stated the names of those on board. Andi was standing beside Miriam watching through the shutters. He looked decidedly like a cave man. When he grunted, she was convinced he might be convincing evidence that Darwin's theory of evolution was being enacted before her eyes.

"Ya Gartery's widow?" he grunted. "He owes us. We have signed papers by him state'n his debts. They've been accumulatin' interest and you be obliged to pay." McCoster spoke in a continuous drawl, without pausing. "We be returning a week from now, and if ye not have the means to pay – we be taking yar house." The others grunted in agreement, and another man stepped forward and shoved another paper into her arms – a list of names and numbers. She saw James' signature at the bottom. These were gambling debts.

"But gentlemen, this is the first I have heard of these debts. I have no reasonable prospect to pay what is owed in one week." She didn't even know the sum… but one week with nothing, made the smallest amount an impossible goal.

The hairy caveman moved towards her, threatening – dragging his knuckles forward. "That ain't our problem. We've been waiting a long time, and now he's dead we ain't waiting no more…"

Jo pushed open the door, anger steaming out of every orifice in her head. She held Miriam's musket in her hand, the barrel shaking slightly. "You've served your request; now you can go!"

Miriam followed close behind her and took the gun from Jo's hand with great purposefulness. "You heard her. Take your leave – the way you came," she said icily, and she blasted the ground at their feet to reinforce her meaning.

* * *

Polly sat at the table. She had allowed the candle to burn low. She'd lost track of the hour. She laid out the documents: the Governor's notification of James' death, the notice in the gazette that told of *The Helena* going down that accompanied a list of those lost, and then the handwritten ledger of creditors and amounts. Somehow this puzzle should all fit together and not be impossible to solve. But as Polly looked from one to the other, she could see no way out. If they took her house, if she was reduced to the street, how would she provide for Jane, Andi, and Jo? Miriam and Bridget could go back to Mrs Thornton's, but suddenly she was very averse to breaking up her family again.

If she had time, there were things she could do. She could take in laundry, or she could get a position like Miriam's. But there was no time and begging for more time didn't offer much hope for leniency. In the end she just spread her hands over the letters. "God," she prayed, "You call yourself husband to the widow, and father to the fatherless. We be needing your provision, because the only bequest James has left us is a pile of debts."

Percy came by the next day. He could feel the sombre tone that permeated the household. As Jane sat shyly by watching him sort things ready for his trip into market, she told him of the visit from the ugly men with the papers. Ugly men must feel comfortable here, Percy thought wryly. He smiled at the little blond-haired princess. How he would love to come riding up on a gallant steed and save her mother-Queen from the evil forces at play. But his hands were tied. Until Polly approached him, there was nothing he could realistically do; and he suspected she would never ask.

He waited. Normally he would stay one or two nights, but this week, he created extraordinarily pressing business that meant he needed to stay much longer. At night he paced up and down outside in the dark. He could not understand Polly. *Stubborn, independent, hard-nosed, arrogant, stiff-necked woman! Would she jeopardise her whole family for the sake of asking? Have I not shown her I am willing and able to help? Have I ever taken advantage of her — even when she was most vulnerable? Am I so revolting to her?*

He stopped mid-stride. The thought hit him like a blow to the stomach. Is that why he found this so distressing? Did it matter so much what Polly thought? He sat down on a rock stunned, examining his intentions over and over. *God! She only found out this week she was widowed. Am I hovering like a vulture over a carcass, lying in wait like her husband's creditors?* All he knew was that there was growing in his heart much more than neighbourly regard. He would stay until Saturday, and if she still could not approach him, he would speak with her. He had to at least give her an option.

Saturday came. It had been impossible to think of anything except the demands of the letters that sat folded in her prayer book. She did not know what to do. She had no way of knowing where to start. Percy had been around, which was odd, but comforting in a way. Jane had such a liking for him, which she thought was nice. There had not been many reliable men in Jane's life. She appreciated that about Percy. He was dependable... and she didn't need to supervise his involvement in their lives. He was just there.

But she didn't think that much about him. She had enough to think about just now. Not one moment passed when those letters did not confront her mind with their awful purpose. As she looked out the window at the muted colours of dusk, she realised something quite momentous. She had not sunk. She was weighed down with the enormity of the threat against her – yes. But she had not gone under! She was still swimming strong, even though the sharks were circling. They were even going to pummel her body, but Jo's escape was like a prophetic word of comfort. No harm would come. Wherever they ended up, God would see that they were not torn to shreds. Suddenly tears of gratitude welled up within her. "Thank you, God, that you are my strength... when I am weak – then You are strong. Your promises are real! Thank you. Oh, thank you."

A tentative tap on the door jamb interrupted her thoughts. Percy stood there, hair neatly tied, eye patch in place, boots polished. "May I have a word Mrs Gartery?"

"Polly – just call me Polly. I am not his wife anymore," she said, still half looking out the window. She was quite distracted.

Percy cleared his throat. "Jane told me..." He hesitated. He didn't know quite how to proceed. "Jane told me of some visitors…that are coming tomorrow."

Polly turned and looked at him. She said nothing.

"I'm not wanting to intrude Polly, but I am concerned for ye. Have ye the means to be satisfying their demands? Have ye decided what to do?"

Polly looked quite surprised that Percy would be even interested, much less concerned. "I have no way of satisfying them. I have decided to do nothing… because that is *all* I can do."

"Nothing? Are you just going to hand yourselves over to this bunch of ruffians?"

"No – just the house," Polly said bluntly. She stood taller, defensive at the implication that she had not thought this through. But thinking did not change the facts. The facts were that she did not have the money and they would evict her… tomorrow. She could not believe the surreal calm that surrounded her.

Percy rubbed his brow and turned away so she would not see his agitation. "Polly, may I speak?"

She looked at him. How strange he was now. Once he would have just said whatever he wanted. "If you must."

"There is a story I been reading in the Bible. It is about a widow whose creditors come demanding payment in full. She went to the prophet Elijah for relief."

She turned her head on the side, trying to work out where he was going with this. She remembered the story – sort of. "And…?"

"And he asked her what she had to sell of value. She had some oil and she borrowed jars to fill up with oil and then she sold it… to pay out her debt."

"They come *tomorrow* Percy. I think I'm even out of oil time."

"You have something you can sell to pay them out."
"Like…."

He swallowed hard. "Your house. If you sold your house, the money would pay them out."

"How does this help me? They may as well just take the house and be done with it."

He turned away again. "Polly – I'm wanting to make an offer on your house. Then you could stay here!"

"*You* want to buy the house out from underneath us?"

"Polly, I cannot just sit by and let this happen! If you pay them their money they cannot come back for more."

She thought again of the shark lurking in the water as the girls played innocently just yards away. It was an analogy of her present circumstances. But right now, she wasn't completely sure whether the shark was Percy or the gambling creditors. "We still will have no home."

Percy sighed. What did she think he wanted with her house? "I would lease it back to you until you can repay the amount – with interest. Then it would be yours again. Fair and square."

Suddenly Polly was hearing him for the first time. "We could keep our home? Really?"

"That is my offer."

"But why? Percy why would you do this for us?" He turned away and shrugged. He said nothing. He was not prepared to expose himself… yet. He was pretty sure Polly was not prepared for it either. But she would not leave it alone. She pushed him for an answer.

"I want nothing Polly, excepting to see ye safe."

"Is there nothing else in exchange for this generosity?"

"I will draw it up legal like, if it suits you."

She was incredulous. She had never encountered such compassion. Even in Percy – who had never been unkind, this extended past the borders of her experience. "Why would ye do this? You are not beholden to us at all Percy Holmes."

"Nor you to me Polly. It is for myself that I do it. I cannot sit by and do nothing when I am in a position to help. You think on it, a while. I have some things to get ready." He left then, and she stared after him in amazement.

Suddenly she saw through the veneer. She stormed after him. "Percival Holmes! You, fraud! You double taking, sneaking, conniving, underhanded brute!"

He turned around and looked at her in shock. What would bring on such a tirade? As she stared him down, he couldn't suppress his smile. This was a Polly he was familiar with.

"Well, don't just stand there in your smug double-breasted merchant's jacket and tell me you have no idea what I'm talking about! If I didn't know better, I'd say you put James Gartery on that ship so you could be free of him yourself."

Not likely, he thought. *There are more efficient means – if I were inclined… which I was – more than once!* Quietly he shook his head. "Murder is a serious accusation Ma'am."

"Okay – you didn't, but you wanted to. You have designs on me becoming your wife. Well, it isn't going to be!"

Percy raised his eyebrows, just slightly. "Polly, I haven't asked you to marry me. I offered to buy your house."

"You don't expect me to marry?" She was so sure she had nailed a motive.

"I don't remember asking." He went into his lean-to and came out with a document. He handed her a piece of paper that set out the proposal of the purchase and leasing conditions in simple, uncomplicated terms. The amount seemed generous, even to her. And if she hadn't been so distraught herself, she would have noticed the paper trembled slightly.

"Oh." Now she felt foolish, and that made her angry. She was mad at her powerlessness. Why couldn't she just do all this by herself? As she looked at the paper and tried to read the terms of his proposal, the words just swam. She trusted Percy. She was pretty sure of that. It's just that this threatened her independence and her need to look after herself and her family, because no one, however well intentioned, could love them as well as her. "Where do I sign?" she said gruffly.

They took it inside, handed her a quill, and directed her to sign at the bottom, and he signed underneath her name. Miriam acted as a witness. And when it was done, he went back to his room and returned with a large leather pouch. It was heavy with coinage. "This is the amount. Ye are to count it out now."

"Why?"

"Because ye need to know I haven't diddled ye…"

"I already know that."

"Count it. I will wait."

"Percy, this is ridiculous! I know ye would be straight." He sat down and waited. She had no alternative but to comply if he was going to leave the house that night. "I know and you know it is correct. No one would ask to have it counted if it was not so. Why do you make such a big deal of it all when it is so late?"

"Because next time, it may not be someone who is straight. It does not hurt to make habits to be thorough, when ye are doing business."

"But it's right! Ye know it!"

"Shortly, you will too." She glared at him again, sparks flying from her eyes. Sometimes he could be so unreasonable! He had overpaid the amount, by one coin. Deliberately – no doubt. She flicked it across the table to him impatiently. And since she was already doing it, she counted out the amounts corresponding on the debt ledger and tied them in small calico pouches with names attached. "When they come tomorrow," said Percy firmly, "give it to them one by one. Watch them count it out and sign that they received their payment. Make sure you have each one witnessed. Keep the copy."

That is what she did. When the mob arrived with their guns, taking their eviction rights seriously, she was poised and collected. She had set a table and a wooden chair on the verandah with a quill and ink well. She rose when they came. "Good morning gentlemen." She went through Percy's procedure with confidence.

They stood bemused, a little in shock. This was not the fun they had expected. A few left when they were given their money. Last of all, McCoster the caveman, stepped forward. He knocked the ink well, splashing it over the front of Polly's dress. She stood up flustered, patting at the ink with a handkerchief in a vain attempt to stop it soaking in. "Gee Mrs Gartery, sorry. Guess I'm not used to these things," said the brute, sniggering at his own cleverness.

Polly looked at him and cringed. There was something about this arrogant barbarian that reminded her of that humiliating day with the collar. She felt her spirit topple and bow down in face of his bullying. She had no more ink. He would come back and harass her as if the settlement had never taken place. Without prompting, words flew to her mind. *"O Lord, let it be thy pleasure to deliver me: make haste, O Lord, to help me. Let them be ashamed, and confounded together, that seek after my soul to destroy it. Let them be driven backward and put to rebuke, they that wish me evil."*

Polly straightened up and looked him squarely in the eye. Inside she felt thrown; outside she stayed calm. "Sir, this presents a dilemma: I have no more ink to record the clearing of my debt. I have no intention of paying you without the prospect of a receipt."

His surliness suddenly turned ugly. "You're gunna pay my money! I've come ready to take ya house and if I need to – I will! You'll be living in ditches with the gutter-rats soon enough!"

"The money is here, Mr McCoster. And it is yours; as soon as you sign a receipt to say you've received the payment in full."

"But ya all out of ink…" he said slyly as if this was her fault and up to her to fix the problem.

"And what would you like me to do about that sir?"

"Ya just might have to give me the money without a signing."

"And risk you coming back for more? I'm sorry, but I don't have the money to pay out a debt more than once."

He leaned over and breathed a fetid blast in her face. "Are you accusing me of cheatin? Just gimme my money or I'll…"

"Don't threaten me sir!" Polly turned her head away in disgust. She sat down and slowly lifted a penknife out of her boot. Hiding it in her hand she brought it around and smoothly held the cold narrow blade against his whiskers. "You look like you be needing a shave, Mr McCoster." She nicked him quickly on the cheek. He started back, shocked and swearing. He held his hand on his face to cover where it bled freely. She passed him the quill. "You're ready to sign now I believe Sir."

He understood her completely, and he swore angrily. He lunged forward, but one of the remaining men pulled his shoulder back. Flushing red, McCoster, shook him lose, dipped the quill in the blood on his hand and made his mark. His companion wordlessly signed beside it, using a drop of blood on the table. He tipped his hat respectfully to Polly and steered McCoster away, who was still cursing her as they left.

* * *

12.

For Polly, it had been a mammoth victory. She had seen some of her old mettle materializing again. But this time it had been different. It emerged out of weakness, and reliance on an ingenuity that was not hers alone. It gave her courage to depend even further on the resources God offered her.

But now Polly was in debt, and there were decisions that had to be made. She needed to pay Percy back his money. She decided to combine this necessity with pursuing Miriam's dream: a school for girls. Polly had been doing this very thing for a long time: teaching life skills to girls. Seeing the confidence and delight her own girls got from reading and writing, she wanted to add literacy into what she did.

Polly opened up to her family about what she was thinking, and they released more ideas to let the dream soar. They talked about who could enrol in the school, how it would be run, what duties needed to be done and when. They would continue to use the lean-to that Percy had put over their little outside classroom and decided a separate building, purpose built with all the things a school would need, was the long-term plan.

Miriam wrote down idea after idea, costing up the concept in her naturally systematic way. Andi suggested that because of the benefits to the emerging colony, the Governor's endorsement to the proposal would give credibility and impetus to the project. She helped Polly write up a draft proposal. Jo and Bridget delivered letters inviting expressions of interest to families around the settlement, outlining the school's objectives and fees. Their enthusiasm was like opening the door to a cage and letting out a bird so it could fly. Somehow this audacious plan became very possible. It was exciting to see their dream fly higher and higher. They would start constructing the schoolhouse with what was left from the sale of the house.

They worked out that if they could get ten paying sponsored positions they could start. Polly was very keen to have at least half that number again in scholarships for girls who had no family to pay for them. Still, very few enquiries trickled back in response to their circulars. Some thought it was an enormous waste of time and resources – a school for *girls*, and even when it was explained that their program would be very practical.

After tea Andi came and sat with Polly on the narrow verandah. They watched a huge flock of top-knot pigeons swoop in a giant grey cloud, darkening the horizon as they in flew in unison over the evening treetops. "I've never seen so many birds together," said Andi. "There must be thousands of them…"

Polly looked at her quizzically. "They are very common. They always fly in flocks like that."

Something tugged at Andi's heart. She knew that one day, in about two hundred years, a flock of forty birds would be considered unusual. *'It's such a shame that things change, shrink and then the smallness becomes the normal measure of how things are,'* Andi thought. She paused. "Polly, I was wondering if we had forgotten something…"

"Oh?" Polly scanned her mind over their plans for any detail she may have overlooked. True, she had never done such a thing before, but it seemed to her that together they had covered just about everything.

"I was thinking that Percy might like to know our plans."

"Percy? Why? If he gets his payment, he'll be happy enough."

"Perhaps – but technically, shouldn't he know what we are planning to do with his house? Besides, he might be able to see something we've missed… an outside perspective. He must be very good at business."

"Why do you say that?"

"Well, because he didn't have much of anything when we first met him… and that's not long ago. He paid cash for the house… so he's obviously doing well – don't you think?"

Polly was irritated. That he would take their house was one thing… but that she could get it back was a matter of pride. She didn't want to include Percy in this. She wanted to do this by herself. "No – I never did think about it."

Andi detected the ice fall from Polly's voice. "Well, he's our friend, isn't he?" she said surprised.

"Percy? Sure – a friend."

"Aren't friends supposed to help each other out?"

Polly suppressed a grunt. "Okay – I'll run it passed him when he comes next. We'll keep trying to find our enrolments 'til then."

As Andi left, Polly looked out at the line of scrub that was receding further away in the face of more buildings. There seemed no logical reason why Percy should have this irritating effect on her. Andi was right. He was their friend, a reliable backdrop against which much of her life had been played. She was happy for him to be in the background. But just recently it seemed that he was constantly being pushed to the front, but even she had to admit, Percy wasn't the one pushing forward. He was never one to blow his own trumpet. It didn't make sense and she wanted to ignore the whole thing. Hopefully then everything would go back to the way things were – when he would drop in with supplies, scruffy and smelly, with no strings attached. He was more comfortable then. This new Percy was harder to fathom.

The day Percy came by, they received word the Governor desired an interview regarding this proposed Girls' School. Polly was pacing nervously like an animal penned for execution. She walked back and forth, her heart pounding in her chest. She had never been on such an official deputation before, and her performance held their future in her hands. She tried to play word-games with her mind, to convince herself it didn't matter too much if she failed. But the truth screamed back at her. It did matter – very much! Everything they had planned and hoped for would pivot on her short reception with the Governor. If he vetoed their proposal, that would kill it. She paced – up and back, up and back, rubbing her temple in agitation. She turned around again and stood staring into the face of Percy.

"What are you doing here?" she accused, jumping nervously.

"I board here periodically... remember?" he said calmly. "I came in to pay what's due."

She looked at him shaking her head in confusion. "Percy, the house is yours. How can you pay me lodging?"

"The leasing arrangements are completely unrelated. I still need a place to stay. And because you keep the room free for me, you can't rent it to someone else who could pay you board. Besides, you cook me meals..."

"From food you bring..."

"... that you pay for by doing my laundry chores. So, I figure if I pay you for lodging, that makes us even."

She pursed her lips. She didn't want to be in anyone's debt anymore. She took the money and counted it out... to appease his fickle, precise ways. "There is more money here than usual. You have over paid."

"Well, I made some enquiries, regarding other lodging. It is much more than what I pay here. I have split the difference. I don't want to underpay for your services... and I still come out better off."

Polly narrowed her eyes and looked at him. Just now it was impossible to pursue finding a hole in his argument. She shook her head in despair and waved him away with her hand.

Percy closed his eye. Would she dismiss him so offhandedly? She was obviously agitated about something of importance. He didn't move.

Polly turned around to see him still standing there. "What?" she said impatiently.

"Just wondered if I could help. Are the creditors coming back?"

"Who?"

"Are there more debts you didn't know about?"

She laughed a tight, nervous laugh. "No, but even if there were, I have no more houses to sell you."

"No debts then – that's good news."

"There is nothing here for you to fix Percy. It is okay. I will work it out."

"So that's it."

"What's it?"

"You think I am here as your self-appointed fix-it man? Did it ever occur to you Polly, I just what to share what is going on in my friend's life?"

She turned back to him stunned. Even after what Andi had said, she had not taken the notion seriously. "Okay. Okay. Andi suggested it. I was getting around to it. You just make it so hard!"

"What is hard? Me being interested?"

"No… Oh blast it all Percy – you are so irritating!"

"Oh, come on... you are Princess Prickles herself. The barbs keep getting sharper by the moment. What have I done?"

"You! You are always so…. so…"

"Forget it, Polly. Forget I asked to be included. You work it out… and I'm not talking about your agitating problems!" He turned on his heel and slammed the door behind him.

* * *

The man at the desk ignored her. He sat shuffling papers, so Polly definitely got the message that there were many other important matters to which the Governor needed to give his attention. Polly smoothed her skirt over and adjusted her detachable lace collar. "His Excellency the Governor will see you now," he said. It was beyond his comprehension why His Excellency would seriously be bothered. Surely the man could delegate these common appointments.

As the door opened, the Governor came forward and politely showed her to a chair. Polly looked in awe at this man of whom she had heard so much.

"Your Excellency, thank you for showing interest in our proposal," began Polly nervously. He looked at her over the braids and bold polished silver buttons that trailed down the front of his jacket.

"Mrs Gartery…" and then he paused. "Have we met? Your name seems familiar to me." Even as he said it, he knew he probably would have remembered this tall lady with the auburn hair if they *had* met before.

"No sir, we haven't met. But I received a letter not long ago from your office, regarding the death of my husband – on *The Helena*."

"Oh of course, Gartery – *The Helena*," he said making the connection. "Ahh, yes… it turned out that your husband also deserted his commission." Polly flinched in horror at the extent of his crime. "Relax, Mrs Gartery – there is nothing to be done. It seems God has seen to justice. It doesn't pay to run from responsibility… especially on the sea, so it seems… it could be the story of Jonah all over again."

His clever attempt at being witty, fell hopelessly flat. Polly shook her head in dismay. "Jonah… and the whale?" He looked at her. It was a poor analogy. He should not have brought it up. Polly took a deep breath. "You don't suppose that he's…" she suggested tentatively. The words could have sounded hopeful, but as the Governor looked at this widow, with raw fear and dread dawning on her face, he guessed the truth about this deserter, and he felt no pity for his plight.

"Saved by a passing whale? No Mrs Gartery, there is no evidence for that at all. Apparently, the storm was a particularly vicious one. It lasted a week. As I remember, a friend of yours – Holmes, was most distressed at the news."

"Percy – distressed?" she said suddenly, quite shocked, but then realised her outburst lacked the formality the situation required. She covered her mouth and blushed quite keenly. There he was again. Even when he wasn't around, Percy made things awkward.

"He struck me as quite a genuine fellow in these times," the Governor said cordially.

"Oh, excuse me Sir, we are not here to talk about my friends, but your interest in the proposal of the girls' finishing school."

"Quite so… moving on then… The School. Yes, interesting indeed. I wanted to commend you in your venture. It shows a great deal of endeavour and foresight to want to pursue such a project… and that is to be encouraged." Polly raised her eyebrows slightly. She had not anticipated such wholehearted endorsement. "However, I'm not sure you understand the enormity of what you are proposing. It is true, right from the establishment of the colony, school enrolments have been available to children of every layer of society: free-settlers, military families, native born and convicts. But the idea of a Finishing School – exclusively for young ladies, I fear there is an element in the colony that will fight this tooth and nail. They are what the emancipists have coined the 'Bunyip Aristocracy' so named after the mythical Aboriginal swamp creature – and it is true... they are a myth. Those with genuine nobility, are not at all threatened by this persuasive lot. Do not be fooled Mrs Gartery, either way, they will not want their daughters mixing with those requiring the assistance of a charitable scholarship to attend. What I fear is that all the good you intend, will lose its support, by that one very basic aspect of your proposal – having a mixed enrolment arrangement. You need the paying students to make it viable, but you will lose them if you include the others."

Polly sat there, unable to take in what he was saying. The school would not... could not, function on her most basic tenet of operation – that education should be available to all. She blinked hard. How could this be? She would not give up her dream. She would not! "You seem very sure of this Your Excellency. Do you think you may have underestimated the worth of their daughters' education? There are few other facilities available in the colony."

"Oh, you are right Mrs Gartery. There is little else outside private tutoring by governesses for young ladies. However, educating girls once they reach a level of basic education, is still considered a luxury that many do not deem necessary. And those who do choose to, usually do so on a very exclusive basis. Believe me – I support your proposal wholeheartedly. The future of this colony is dependent on the establishment of solid families and educated adults. How better than to embed this with young women at such a school? It is a project of immense foresight and credibility."

Polly sighed. "But. There is always a 'but'…"

He smiled a wry smile. "I have found with politics, that the 'buts' usually get bigger with the audaciousness of the plan. Please do not let this information deter you Mrs Gartery. I also know that with every 'but' there is usually another way to serve the purposes you propose. It is just a matter of factoring it in." He stood and extended his hand. "Thank you for your time, Mrs Gartery and sharing your vision with me. I trust you will find a way round. I will be most interested to hear how you go."

Polly stood and nodded her appreciation. All the way home, she went over every detail of that interview. What a remarkable man. She wondered how a person of his standing could leave her feeling that *he* had been the one privileged to be privy to her dreams and plans.

What she could not understand, was how she could have failed to account for all the prejudice and bigotry she endured every day of her life. She knew from experience they could be downright brutal. Why did she ignore the fact that the girls grew up in these families who would not be any different? These families voted with their feet. They would walk out the door, taking their daughters and fees with them, especially if something didn't suit. She knew the Governor was right. It would not work. *"God,"* she cried in her heart, *"how could You give me this beautiful dream and then scratch it and pummel it and knock it around, until it resembles nothing like the original gem."* She felt cheated and angry. Was it always hopeless to want more?

What else had the Governor said? "With every 'but' there is another way. It is a matter of factoring it in…"

Suddenly she felt she was standing in the courtroom dock all over again. She was charged and found guilty. She blamed God for the failure of her dream before it even got off the ground. She sighed as another thought racked her mind. *Was the only proof that God was in something, was a lack of obstacles?* Surely if something was worthwhile, it was natural that there would be frustrations along the way. There must be a way forward… there must be.

* * *

Polly soberly sat down with the girls. They were waiting to hear what the Governor had said. Andi made a little cough. "Didn't he want a girl's school in the colony?"

Polly was jolted out of her thoughts. "Oh no, he was very supportive. He couldn't say enough good things about the idea. *'A project of immense insight and credibility'* is the way he put it I think…" Her voice trailed off as the girls erupted into cheers.

"Yes!" congratulated Jo as she high-fived all hands in her vicinity! "That is just what we prayed for… that he would see the significance of what we are planning, *and* he would be supportive!"

Andi paused and glanced at Polly. It was evident she was not at all excited by the Governor's words. "I don't understand – why you aren't pleased? I thought the Governor's support is exactly what we needed to see this to the next stage."

Polly braced herself as the girls quickly became quiet. "So, did I. However, I think he called the interview to ensure I was taking into account some things…"

"What sort of things?" asked Miriam concerned. They had clearly overlooked some necessary data.

"He believes we will encounter opposition once the basis of the school's operation becomes better known. He has grave concerns that it will self-destruct. I agree with him."

"I don't understand; what do you mean?" said Jo seriously.

"Well, he believes – as we have planned it – that the school won't work. Those who afford the fees, which we need to make the school viable, will not want their daughters educated with those who can't. He believes it will fall apart if we try to make that the basis of operating the school."

Bridget stomped her feet. "They can't tell us how we run our school! That is so unfair. I can read! That's just because Andi believed I could and taught me without making me pay for it. How can they say I should not learn to read! What about the others like me? Where do they get their chance?" Angry tears smarted her eyes.

Polly raised her eyebrows. She thought it was an honest summary of what everyone was feeling.

Polly shifted in her seat, as something tugged at her mind. *"Be angry, and do not sin…"* Where had she heard that? Mary-Jane, her nurse had said that. *"Feel the injustice,"* she would say, *"be angry – but don't sink into self-indulgence."* Polly could feel the rising indignation starting to degenerate without restraint.

"Girls, girls… hush – I know what you are saying. I have been saying these same things to myself over and over. But that is not all the Governor said. He also said that with every problem there is usually another way to serve our purposes. We just have to factor it in. He wants us to find a way. He can't do that for us. If the school is a good idea… a God-idea… then there will be a way. The school has to pay. We cannot afford to do what our hearts would like and charge no fees at all. So, there must be another way to do the same thing. I don't know what it is… but if we believe God knows everything, he will also have a solution. But to hear that solution we can't start indulging our anger."

Polly bowed her head. "Father, this school is Thine. Help us to factor this in. We want to make this school one that provides opportunities for others, like the opportunities that have been given to us. Amen."

They went about their evening chores, quietly praying for solutions to emerge that would provide a way to fulfil the dream.

* * *

13.

Percy periodically came in from the bush and stayed in the rough outside room. He rarely made attempts to see or talk to Polly. Sometimes he came late and left so early, she did not even know he had been there until she found a small leather pouch with her rent money in it, sitting on the old scarred sideboard. She started repaying her debt in the same fashion – hanging the pouch on a nail by the door to his lean-to. And when they did meet, those times were awkward.

Polly took in laundry until the school became a reality. It was hard, knuckle-breaking work. The labour she had done as a convict in the women's factory was easier. But this work kept her independent... one step ahead and that gave laundry an edge that factory labour never could boast.

The girls did laundry collections in the morning and then returned the sheets and clothes in big baskets to the houses in the evening. In between delivery times, they did the washing. They did most of the work down by the creek to save carting water. They scrubbed and boiled and starched and steamed. But they also set their minds towards their dream. Miriam spent the many hours over soapsuds reading and studying: her books propped on a branch away from the water. Bridget used the time learning numbers, counting and adding while chopping wood for the boiler and carrying buckets of water from the creek to the house. Andi taught them lessons practically applying spelling and problems as they folded and sorted. No second was wasted. The dream did not die... it stayed alive – cocooned, safe and growing, while the practical issues of surviving were addressed. If nothing else, their laundry service became quite sort after. Even Eliza Thornton took advantage of it.

One evening when Polly was doing the deliveries Mrs Thornton came to the door herself when she knocked. "Mrs Gartery it is impossible for me to find good help. It is easier just not to bother. Your laundry service is commendable." She paused and then rushed on, so the effect of her lavish praise was not wasted. "Do you think Miriam would consider coming back on a live-in basis?"

"Miriam is entirely at her own bidding, Mrs Thornton. Even though she is truly part of our family, what she decides is up to her."

"Perhaps you could speak with her… to offer some influence on my behalf?"

Polly looked at her. Now why would she do that? "Mrs Thornton, have you considered having other girls who are trained to do Miriam's work?"

"Oh of course I've tried. There is no one – not with her skills. That girl is unique. A one and only." Eliza sighed dramatically. She wanted Mrs Gartery to come compassionately to her aid and hand Miriam back. It annoyed her she was not cooperating. Eliza really didn't want to admit to any living soul she might have to work herself. Yet it had even come to that… once or twice.

"Mrs Thornton, I would beg to differ. Miriam is no different from many other girls, even the ones you have already tried… except for one thing… one thing only."

"That is not so. Miriam is above them by leagues. It is insulting to say she is common. Why – she can even read," Eliza said as her concluding argument.

"But this is my point. Now she is second to none. In all seriousness she is worth more than people are willing to pay…"

"Are you saying I am not *paying* her enough! Well goodness, why didn't you say so? I would pay double if she'd come back." Eliza looked relieved that such a minor thing would see her regain Miriam's services. She laughed lightly, firmly believing Miriam was within her grasp once again.

"Mrs Thornton, that is *not* what I am saying at all. Miriam has skills and literacy because she has graduated from a finishing school. Any other person could be the same – given that opportunity."

"Finishing school, my bonnet! That is for the distinguished classes… not maids." That was ridiculous.

"Depends on what one is 'Finishing' – I dare say. You said yourself Miriam was without parallel in possessing the skills you require."

"Well yes, but Miriam has outstanding abilities. Besides, no such school exists in the colony to teach these things. I have been unable to find anything available for normal girls, much less what you propose. I know because I looked on behalf of my niece. We ended up paying a fortune to have a private governess brought out from England."

"Oh, but there *is* such a school, Mrs Thornton. The very school that Miriam came through is re-establishing. The Governor is fully supportive of the project."

"Yes well. We all know how discerning he can be." Eliza resented the irritating persistence the Governor had shown in extending social courtesies to those with Freedom Pardons as though they had never been prisoners. They had no right to resume life as freemen. Eliza knew the importance of social standing and it was obvious to her which of those she met were ex-convicts and those who weren't. Mrs Gartery, for example – she was obviously from a lower-class situation, but she would never have been a convict. However, the Governor was a representative of the King, so if he supported Mrs Gartery's rather extraordinary idea, maybe the idea had a little credibility.

Polly ignored the barb about the Governor. "Mrs Thornton, to get the help you need, it would be necessary for you to sponsor a girl's education for a period. Then they would be obliged to give you that equivalent amount of time in service for the privilege of their education. Of course, at the end you could negotiate terms of continuing service for as long as you both agree. Keep in mind, that to have someone in service that is able to read and write well, a longer period of education would be necessary."

Mrs Thornton stood staring. Perhaps this *did* have possibilities. "How long to train a girl ready for service?"

Polly cringed. She thought Eliza Thornton had the diplomacy skills of a warthog. "Really Mrs Thornton, these are not horses to be broken-in for a harness over a weekend. They are girls who need educating, and that takes time. Like you say, some of these girls start knowing very little. Two years of tutoring would be needed at least. But perhaps, knowing how anxious that you are to see the fruits of your investment… they could start in basic service each morning, and return to us for the rest of the time to complete their learning. They will obviously need somewhere to stay during this time."

"And I could have my very own Miriam?" She sounded a little excited, as if she was being offered a merino ram with stud papers.

Polly took a breath. "Miriam is one of our tutors. You can be sure your very own Mary, or Catherine, or whoever she is, will be well taught. You won't lose out. You'll know exactly when they will be with you because it has all been pre-arranged. After that contracted time, they'll be free to go elsewhere if that is their wish."

"Did you say Miriam is one of *your* tutors? This is *your* school? I have not heard this before," said Eliza reproachfully.

Ahh yes. She had refused to respond when they had approached her previously. "We are only just starting to publicise our offers for positions. The Governor has called it a project of 'immense insight and credibility'. However, you understand, these things move slowly until people are made aware," reflected Polly.

"Oh, but you are wrong! I know many ladies who are as equally frustrated as myself. They would be delighted to see how this could aid their situation." Eliza took a deep breath. This was a promising solution to her problems. "Yes Mrs Gartery," she said decisively, "I will undertake to have three girls. Let me know as soon as possible, so we can organise what you need. When do they start?"

"We really need to have ten enrolments for the first classes to begin. You said you knew of others who would be interested. I'd be happy to go with you to explain the basis for our school."

When Polly got home, she dropped into her leather armchair. She could not quite account for that conversation with Eliza Thornton. Did she actually say those things? It was as if some stitches of a complex tapestry were woven in place, and then other coloured threads had fallen into position around it. Was such a thing possible?

She saw the whole thing clearly. Quickly she went to the table and wrote down the elements of this new strategy. It seemed so remarkably plain. She pinched herself and went outside to splash cold water from a wooden pail over her face. She gasped as the water trickled down her shoulders.

Andi and Jo arrived back from their deliveries just as Polly plunged her whole head into the bucket. Polly saw the girls holding each other's hand, staring at her, as she came up gasping for air. Had the stress caused her to lose stability once more? Were they going to relive the agony of her sickness all over again?

Polly danced over to them, bubbling over with laughter, her dress dripping, her hair falling undone, and spun them around lightly. "Pinch me so that I can be absolutely certain I'm awake!" Polly demanded of Jo who looked intensely into her face, because quite seriously, Jo wasn't sure everything was okay.

Jo saw the delight and twinkle in Polly's eyes and burst out laughing. "Yes – you're awake! In fact, you look like you've woken up like Rip van Winkle. Tell us! What has happened?"

"The school! Our school! A way has been made around the 'but'... I'm sure of it!"

Whoops of delight and congratulations rang out around the trees. Some neighbours came out and looked on dubiously as they spontaneously danced around the cooking pot. It was a victory dance like the one in the Bible, when Moses' sister Miriam, danced after the Red Sea parted so the Israelites could escape from being attacked by Egyptians. God had performed a miracle today. He had made a way where there was no way... and they had to celebrate.

* * *

14.

In two weeks, Polly had signed on the registrations that they needed to start the school. Polly's contacts in the colony meant finding students to enrol was the easy part now that they had shifted their focus from finishing school to apprenticing staff. Each evening after dinner she paced around the sitting room, constantly in motion. It helped her think. Every so often she would stop at the table and abruptly sit down and scrawl something on a sheet of paper. Then she would stand up and start orbiting again, gently rubbing her temple with two fingers. Finally, Andi was dizzy from watching her circle and went outside.

She saw a candle alight in Percy's room, and she knocked tentatively on the open door. Jo and Bridget were already there, sitting on a large red Kangaroo skin on the floor chatting to him about the progressing school plans. Andi sat on a rough three-legged stool.

Percy was pleased that their endeavour was becoming a reality. He was proud of their boldness to fight for success. But it also seemed that the closer they got to fulfilling this dream, the more remote his part in their lives was destined to become. That grieved him. The loss was already too real.

How was it that the girls could always sense he was here and came to chat about what was happening, yet Polly was completely oblivious to his comings and goings? He was invisible to her; he was sure of it. Perhaps there was a blindness that lingered in her heart; the blindness he had prayed healing for. He continued to pray; and was prepared to remain invisible until her sight was fully restored. Percy was well aware that moment would unveil the truth. What if she did finally see him and still turned away? He'll leave then, if she still locked him out, but she had to *see* him first.

Andi looked at Percy's hands, busy plaiting leather strands into wide, flat, versatile braided straps. "Polly's wearing a track around the room in there. She stops to write something down and then she starts again. I was getting dizzy, so I came outside…"

Percy nodded a bit, his hands automatically weaving and threading the fine leather strips. "She's goat-tracking, huh?" He stopped momentarily to wipe his brow that beaded with perspiration.

"Call it what you like; it's exhausting watching her like that."

"Yep – it's that, all right," said Percy. "She's… that's her way for processing. Ain't seen her doin' it for a long time though." He sounded relieved that normality was resuming once more. "Anytime there have been big things a foot, she would goat-track, sometimes for hours. Just walking around and rubbin' her head like it keeps the ideas a-flowing." He smiled again, a soft, affectionate smile.

The candlelight flickered as he paused his leatherwork. He arms felt heavy and he was sweating. Jo looked at him in concern. He looked sick. "Are you okay? I mean… you look like you're going to throw up…and you're shaking." Jo stared at his hard, brown hands that had stopped work. There was a distinct tremble in them.

Andi saw it too. "Did you eat anything tonight?" Her Gran would shake like that if she skipped a meal… but she was old – much older than Percy.

Percy jolted back to reality. He had a room full of girls staring at him. He did feel a bit crook. He had forgotten to eat… not that that was unusual. He didn't always have the luxury of a meal every day. Andi quickly volunteered. "I'll get something for you… and make some tea." She went out to stoke the fire and pulled her shawl in around her. The evening breeze had a coolness about it.

"Just the tea… I don't feel so hungry…" He put down his leatherwork. He felt tired… and hot. Tonight, was unseasonably warm, he thought. Andi brought him a mug of watery tea. The tea-leaves had to be used again and again. Still… tea in any form tasted good. He could get used to these sorts of homely comforts. He sipped it gratefully. "I might turn in Girls. I'm dead beat and I've an early start. Take care of each other and keep going with your plans. It's good to see it all coming together."

He smiled wanly as they said goodnight and filed out. He couldn't believe how blessed he was. They were great kids – a surrogate family given to him in place of his real family; young sisters and brothers he had badly neglected back home. He pictured the small, thatched cottage nestled in a row of similar cottages, overlooking the emerald-hedged wolds of Lincolnshire. It was all so foreign to him now… except the faces seated at the table. He held them in his imagination and he looked around at each one… suspended in time as he saw them last: the work-weary hands of his father, clasped in prayer... the grubby little faces of his twin brothers as they pulled frogs captured from the village pond out of their pockets, and put them on the chair of his middle sister, waiting for the screams as they jumped on her grimy pinafore... the wilted daisy chain around his youngest sister's neck... and the twinkle in the eye of Grandma Hetty, sharing a secret with the two older girls as they served the meal. Percy prayed then for each of his family. He knew they would all be grown now... the passage of years does that... and he would never know how they were going, if they were well, or if they were not... but he prayed anyway and trusted God to reach over the million miles that separated them and touch them with His grace... knowing somewhere in the middle, their prayers would meet his on a return journey across the seas.

Suddenly he had an urgency to write... to pen a letter and let them know that he was alive and safe. All these years and they never even knew if he survived the journey on that dank prison hulk. Why had he never thought of this before? Something so simple. He almost decided to do it immediately, but he lay down on his stretcher and closed his eyes. He would write it in the morning before he left... and a short detour to the wharf would see it delivered.

* * *

15.

"Andi! Wake up!" Jo shook her friend by the shoulder in the dark. "Wake up! You need to come. Andi!" Andi stirred groggily. It was pitch black, and silent – with the silence of deep night. Jo shook her again, persistent, and urgent. "Come on Andi... get up!"

Andi sat up and knocked her head hard on the bunk above her. Every morning she wanted to rip out these revolting bunks and replace them with ones that were a civilized height with real mattresses. But then, at the end of every day she was so exhausted that even these lumpy, cramped beds were a relief... until morning arrived. "Ouch!" Andi struggled out of bed, as she rubbed her forehead.

Jo threw her shawl around her shoulders. "Quick! Come with me." Jo dragged her by the arm out the back to Percy's room. A candle sat on a box beside his stretcher, flickering on its last stump of wax. Percy lay on his side, curled and groaning in pain. His hair and shirt drenched in sweat, his eye patch discarded, his lip bleeding where he had bitten down in a spasm of agony.

Andi stood staring at him in shock. "Jo! He is really sick! Quick – get Polly... Miriam... anyone!"

"I wasn't sure I should wake them."

"Go on! I don't know what to do! O God! What do we do?" Jo left in a hurry as Andi went outside to the covered pail and dipped out some water into a basin. She squeezed out a clean rag and ran it across his forehead. She grabbed a mug and tried to give him a drink. His good eye was glassy with fever, yet he seemed to understand what she wanted and drank thirstily. Abruptly a spasm of pain grabbed him in its vice, and he knocked the mug flying as he clenched the side of the stretcher hard in his hands. The veins in his neck extended as he bit down and fresh blood oozed from the cut on his lip.

Polly and Miriam appeared at the door. They stood there momentarily before they flew into motion. They waited for the spasms to pause and then helped him onto the floor mat. There he had room to stretch and thrash with less danger of hurting himself. Miriam and Jo carried his bunk outside to allow more room in the tiny space and went to the wood heap with a broom handle and axed off a length of smooth rod. She brought it back and placed it across his mouth. Jo looked totally bewildered, but as the next spasm took hold, he bit down hard on the wood, sparing his lip. Miriam had more sticks on hand. It would not be long before he'd bite these in two. Polly stripped the few blankets off the bunks inside the house and piled them over his body, sponging the sweat pouring off his face.

"His skin's boiling. Shouldn't we take the blankets off?" asked Andi concerned.

"We have to get the fever to break," said Polly weakly. She had seen such fevers – with the pain that came in waves, spasms wracking the body. It did not bode well.

"But my mother would say that when my brother had fevers that we needed to cool him down… take his clothes off, sponge him – without making him shiver," said Jo anxiously.

Polly shook her head, staring at Percy lying there glazed in fever, muttering deliriously, extending his neck as he muffled a gut-wrenching cry when a spasm came. Now was not the time to experiment with new ideas about trying to cool a fever down. She had always done it this way. Mims went and got a fresh candle.

"Can't we get a doctor? Couldn't they give him something for the pain?" asked Andi, tears welling in her eyes.

"There is nothing... nothing to be done but to wait and pray," said Polly as she wiped his forehead again. "We can always pray." A sob caught in her throat, as she removed the blankets, and sponged his face. For a moment he seemed to settle. How could this be Percy lying here? Percy was invincible. Yes, he wore scars and wounds from battles he had fought, but he always came through. Percy was the one with solutions, not problems. He had more answers than she cared to have questions. He never needed her, even after the death of his wife; he never spoke about Burilda or what happened. She had gleaned just basic information from the girls. And he needed her less since he had cleaned up and was proving himself a force in this fledgling colony. This was not happening! She couldn't remember her life in the Colony without him. He should always be here! Percy rolled over and spat the stick out of his mouth... and vomited in the bowl she held. And then he screamed as the pain revisited with vengeance.

Polly gave Miriam the cloth and quickly went outside. She leant over behind the outside long-drop toilet and was sick. She weakly leant up against the rough timber frame, as the crescent moon made its thin rise over the trees. Percy. Percy. She saw in her mind the thousand times she had brushed him away when he reached out to her. She saw with shame the cold distance and the harsh accusations she threw at him. Why would she do that? Were friends so plentiful, that she could afford to abuse the few faithful ones God had placed in her circle?

"Oh God, forgive me. I have been so desperate to be independent and need no one. This man is not James. I know that. He has shown me that over and over. Why would I punish him for the sins of another man? He has made no demands on me... except for requesting friendship. I could not even offer him that. Oh, dear Jesus... forgive me... I did not know what I did!" Her heart shattered as she saw the enormity of her fear. And she remembered those words read to her over and over, imprinted on her subconscious: *Perfect love casts out fear.*

"How can I ever love, when I have known so much fear?" But even as she said it, she realised she had it back to front. God's love evicts fear. Only God's perfect love was big enough to insulate her heart in the face of such hurt. "But God, my heart is so sore! I know You are showing me your love – every day, in millions of little ways. I want to be able to return such friendship, but I am scared. Will I ever grow strong enough to take such a step? Will I ever have the chance now? Will you take him away before I can accept such a gift from his hand?"

Sobs broke again from her heart. "Spare him! Please... God... You must do it. I have seen these fevers... without You, he will not come through! Spare him to..." and with sadness Polly realised he had grown into the person God designed him to be... more than she'd ever dare admit. "Oh God, if you have no desire to spare him, even if you want him for yourself... spare me the loss his going will cause. Please God. Please."

Eventually Polly wiped her face and went back inside. Her family clustered around his blankets on the floor, praying. They understood there was little else they could do. Miriam sponged his face and offered sips of water... and the others quietly wept their prayers to God. To the Father – who spoke to create life; to Jesus – who healed all sorts of sickness when he walked on earth; to the Holy Spirit – who raised people from the dead and made lame men walk in the early history pages of the church. He is the comforter, and they clung to Him in desperation. They had no one else to turn to. It was an impossible thing to expect them to sleep, or eat, or do something. They just knelt there, their faces wet with tears and exhaustion taking its toll. Somehow, they knew that by morning they would know the answer.

* * *

The night crawled by. Darkness deepened and Percy no longer writhed in spasmodic pain, but lay exhausted, groaning persistently as a constant throbbing tormented his body. He called out to Grandma Hetty and his sisters when the fever took hold again and sent him hallucinating back to the scenes of his childhood. Slowly the black night gave way to the predawn grey that crept in through the slits between the rough timbered walls. He dozed fitfully.

With the clean rays of sun bursting through the slats in that primitive room, fresh hope filled the vigil-keepers. As morning rose further, Polly sent the girls out to have a bite to eat and start the laundry rounds. They still had obligations to fulfil.

She stayed by his side for two days, barely eating or sleeping, cleaning the small room with fastidious care after each bout of sickness, and in between his delirious muttering. Polly barely knew this room. She never came here. It was frugal in its furnishings: one shipping crate as a table, one box where his candle stood and another that also doubled for a chair. There was a low three-legged stool and a kangaroo rug on the floor. There was a thick handmade nail that hung his hat and razor strap, and a wooden peg for his blanket swag. Now, instead of feeling that a man who needed so little was deficient in his heart, she admired its rough simplicity. It was not that he was unable to appreciate beautiful things – hadn't he made her soft armchair? It puzzled her that one person could choose an environment so devoid of comfort – however meagre.

As she could see him settling Polly reluctantly relinquished his care to Bridget and took over the back wrenching work down by the creek. Dunking linen in the boiler with a long pole. It reminded Andi of a gondola pole used by the gondoliers to navigate the canals of Venice in their flat-bottomed boats. Then they twisted the sheets into long python-snakes squeezing out the excess water before they dragged the baskets back to the house and strung them out to dry. Polly sent Jane, Jo, and Andi, emotionally and physically exhausted, to have a sleep while she finished up the smaller things with Miriam.

Bridget dozed by Percy's bed as he lay sleeping. His head was damp with perspiration, but he no longer doubled up in rigours and pain. He opened his eye and looked around searching for a recollection of what had happened. His head throbbed, his body still groaned in the aftermath of torture, and his tongue cleaved to the roof of his dry mouth. He had been this close to death's door before, and he knew instinctively how close he had been this time. He turned and saw Bridget slumped exhausted over the table. It was one of the young girls who tended him. He had thought… he had hoped… Perhaps it was just the wish of a dying man who had feverishly desired that it had been Polly who faded in and out of his consciousness. That impression had drawn him back… just like Burilda had drawn him back once before. But Polly was not here. His disappointment knew no bounds. So, it was true. Even an appointment with the angel of death could not bring compassion to her heart. There was nothing here after all. It was a mere delusion that a once genuine friendship could revive and grow into something more precious.

As he lay on the floor, covered in blankets washed by her hands, he decided. He knew he had a choice. He could choose to fight the disease that wracked his body… or give in to it. Giving in was not in his nature. While he had breath, he would fight. With God's healing strength he would win. Then he would move on, and let Polly get on pursuing her personal dreams. It was evident there was no room in them for him.

Australia was a big place. He knew that… and now he was not bound by tribal boundaries. The settlers had hardly made inroads at all. He would go west – out along the

Hawkesbury... or even further... and find a space that would be his own. He would give Polly the distance that she so persistently demanded. If there was no other gift she would take from his hand, he could offer this.

* * *

When Polly returned from the laundry run, Percy lay sleeping – motionless and fatigued from his struggle with death. She removed the rugs and again sponged his face and body, running the cloth over the scars along his chest. Tears, tired and strained, blinked in her eyes as she lingered over his face... his mouth, firm and determinedly set. She was certain it was set hard with his will to recover. How could she let this so effortlessly slip through her hands? "Oh Percy," she whispered, "You stubborn, obstinate man – hang in there. Please... don't give up on me now... hang in there..."

She left again and he stirred as she softly closed the door. When she finally lay on her bed late that night, she understood something about herself – she had spent a lifetime prising open doors to survive. She desperately wanted to do it differently now. Particularly with Percy. But she was not certain whether she was to allow this new dream of her heart happen naturally. Or was this something she needed to fight for, to forcefully squeeze on through... obstinately... like Percy. *"Oh God, forgive me. I will try. I will try not to shut him out any longer. The prospect of my life without him seems unbearably barren. Please let this be one dream that survives."*

* * *

16.

Percy lay on his bed for days. The fever and pain returned intermittently, sometimes violently. However, the spells between spasms grew longer and the pain lessened. Bridget always came to get Polly if he relapsed, but those times were rare now. Polly checked in on him before she retired at night and always, he was sleeping the exhausted sleep of a body that was struggling to restore its equilibrium. He was getting better.

Polly longed for the time when she could spend a lucid moment with Percy, but every visit had been frustratingly clouded. But just now she didn't have time to indulge her personal wishes, so she took comfort from the reports he was growing stronger. Laundry seemed to go through cycles of peaks and valleys; and at present there was a whole mountain of work that faced them endlessly. Polly started rotating the girls' duties, so that they could have a break by taking turns in the less strenuous work of nursing Percy. But it also meant an extra load for herself.

Polly contacted her students to start lessons. She had put it off while Percy was critical, but she could not delay it any longer. Besides, to have extra hands while they were snowed under mounds of sheets was a benefit of launching their 'school' immediately. They went down to the creek to do the washing, dragging heavy sodden linen in baskets back to the house to wring and hang on the line. "This is our first lesson: we help each other. So, help Jo with these baskets of linen. Here, take a sheet like this… and twist."

Jo nodded as her partner grabbed the other end. One thing that Jo learnt early on was that work was always work. You could drag it out... or you could try and make it interesting. "I like to think of something that really gets my goat. And then I squeeze really hard," she said.

The girls raised their eyebrows. Each one could think of a million things that made them mad. Most of those things were foul breathed drunks that frequented the tavern. They twisted the sheets with savage grips. Jo laughed. "I don't think we've ever had these sheet wrung out so well. We are going to get through this in record time."

Polly nodded as they struggled to hang the wet items over the line. "You are doing well. When we finish here, I will go over with each of you how we will go about your training. You will have a week to think about whether you want to continue. After that we will go and introduce you to your sponsors."

With increasing confidence Polly stepped into the new routines of the school. Each student was given a thorough explanation of Polly's expectations. Jo and Andi listened through the wall to the spiel given to newcomers and remembered their own introduction to life at Polly's house. Andi whispered to Jo, "I think things have actually changed around here. I didn't think that was possible when we arrived..."

"Oooh yeah," she agreed, "and aren't we glad about that!"

The students were allocated a rotating roster of house duties at their sponsors' home, chores, and lessons in the afternoon at home. Andi happily relinquished laundry duty for reading and writing lessons. Reading was fast becoming Jane's first passion. Finding enough suitable things to read was always a challenge.

When one of the students did not show in the morning, Polly went into a spin. She anxiously searched out what happened to her and found the girl was not sick but had left to marry a settler. Polly didn't begrudge the girl her choice, but how could she possibly reimburse their sponsors' investment if students abandoned their enrolment like this? Shorter, pay-as-you-go blocks seemed safer, so she put in a weekly pay structure. The girls would still undertake their routines of morning work, with classes of instruction each afternoon. That cycle would be repeated for as long as the arrangement was agreeable to both parties. It gave each party an 'out' if things were not working... and she could shuffle for different experiences to round out their training.

Polly slowed the number of laundry jobs she was taking in, so the girls could devote time to studies. She worried that her financial commitments to Percy might stall because of that decision, but she hadn't wanted to talk business with him until he was well. Over the last couple of busy days, she had seen him increasingly out and about and she knew that the time was now.

* * *

Percy penned the letter to his family. With tenderness he told them of his recent sickness and now he was recovered. He explained very little of his past life, except to say that he had been granted his freedom, had been married, but his wife

190

had died. He told them of his new deep faith in God and thanked them for their faithful prayers. He assured them of his prayers for them also… and wished them every blessing. As he signed it, he sealed it with a kiss. His family deserved much better than he had given them. He was sorry, so sorry for the grief he had caused them.

He reached out and took a clean sheet of paper. He had written this letter to Polly many times in his mind as he lay on his bed. The words were well rehearsed and came automatically as he wrote them down. He tried not to think beyond what had to be explained. Then he picked up another sheet, restoring full ownership of the house to Polly, and folded it inside. He wrote her name on the outside and laid it on the table. He would leave early in the morning. He had spoken with the girls during the day and said goodbye. They knew he would be going on a trip on the morrow. They didn't know he intended not to come back. He stalled. He was hoping against hope that it didn't have to be… but what was the use in waiting for the hopeless?

He picked up the letter to his family. Tonight, he would take it to the wharf and see it safely delivered to a courier. In the bright light of a clear moon, he walked to the wharf and back again. It tired him, but he was so wound up he could not contemplate going to sleep. He sat in the shadows of the moonlight and wondered if he should just leave tonight, but he wanted to give it one last chance.

* * *

After tea Polly went out to Percy's room and knocked. There was no answer. She pushed open the door to find his swag rolled and his ink well and quill on the table. A piece of paper was folded with her name written on the outside. Polly sat down on the upturned crate and picked up the paper. Her hand trembled as she held it. Why would Percy be writing her? He hadn't gone yet – his swag was still propped in the corner… but she sensed he was getting well enough to attempt another trip. She relaxed… perhaps he just wanted to pay a nursing fee or some silly thing. But as she looked at the folded paper, and the careful print on the outside… she could not bring herself to open it. Fear began to grow in her heart. A different fear to what she was familiar with, an apprehension that she would never see a special dream come true.

She looked at the folded paper in her hand for a long time. It seemed to distend... becoming larger than life… until she finally took a deep breath. She unfolded it quickly closing her eyes against her fear. A loose sheet of paper fell, unnoticed under the table into the shadows. Polly held the thick paper in her damp hands and read the first line… then she realised all her fears were justified. He *was* going away. Not just for a time, but forever. Why? Why now? Surely, he could hear her change of heart when it was so loud to her own ears! Was that why? Did he feel trapped? Did he think that she would strangle his wanderlust freedom?

Tears fell, unheeded onto the paper splodging the ink. Then disgust came over her. A private loathing, for not being aware enough to realise a how precious something is, before it is too late. She never doubted for a moment that it was too late. Men didn't commit things to paper until they had made up their minds.   And her experience was that men didn't change their minds once they were made up.

* * *

As Percy finally decided to turn in, he noticed a lone pelt pegged onto the outside wall of the cookhouse. He looked at it... knowing full well that if he didn't do anything with it now, it would stay there forever, as a memorial of an unfinished job. That would be a waste... and it was a large pelt, the last he had pegged out before he became sick. Perhaps Polly could use it. Their resources were not so plentiful that they could afford to be wasteful. He took it down and stripped off his shirt as he rubbed and broke the dried skin with a rock in his customary method. The activity helped ease the pain of going... one last token of doing things well and leaving nothing incomplete. In the back of his mind, he tried to believe that Polly would come out to him; that the veil of invisibility would lift. But as he glanced at the house, every so often, it remained still and quiet.

* * *

Polly could hear Percy moving outside.   She sat paralysed. She knew he had not intended her to read the letter until he was gone. She wanted to pretend this was what she wanted, and nothing had changed – that she was unaffected by his decision to go.

She tried to stir herself. Polly struggled to assimilate the truth.   Her breathing came in short gasps as she quickly brushed her eyes. In the letter Percy confessed that he had appointed himself as their guardian while there was need, and now that they were established, his sickness had grown in him a desire to seek new frontiers. Polly went over in her mind the night he was sick, when she first encountered that feeling of loss and grief. It came now in new waves, only this time with finality. Tonight, there was no fear of death stealing him away, but this stolen dream seemed just as final. Polly struggled to her feet. She had waited, hoping he would come in and find her reading the letter, allowing her tears to explain her disappointment, but even that plan was destined to fail. He was obviously avoiding her. She had survived so much in the past. With God's help she could survive this too.

* * *

Time ticked away silently, and with each stroke Percy pushed across the dry, crackled inside of the fur-skin, he looked towards the still dark house again, and realised he waited in vain. Anger and disappointment rose as he pushed harder and faster. Sweat ran across his forehead and under his eye-patch. He ripped it off in disgust and threw it aside as he worked determinedly to see this one final task finished. He would leave no loose ends untied. Not this time. His hair came loose falling about his face in an unruly mass, but he was too focused to notice or care.

Polly stood at the door of his lean-to, mesmerized. She watched Percy's frenzied work, captivated by the sight of his scarred back, his twisted eye, and his matted hair under the eerie glow of moonlight. She remembered those early days when his visits brought the provisions that sustained them day-to-day. She felt all the comfort and security... as his rough, unpolished ways brought her first experience of genuine friendship, based on nothing other than sincere good will and possum stew. Polly understood something then as she stared at this wild picture of the past. She realised that she never trusted Percy's new respectable look. Not really. She saw it as a shallow veneer – that probably covered shallow, cheap tricks to serve shallow, cheap ends. Deep down, she did not believe this new Percy was still the same Percy, with no other agenda, save to be her friend. Yet, here he was... planning to leave on a longed-for journey into new frontiers, and before he went, he needed to see that she had one last pelt, broken and supple, and useable.

Tears of appreciation streamed down her face. Such friendship was unknown to her. It was more than losing the familiar. His going was much, much more than that. She determined that she would try, somehow, to change his mind... to buy time, to make him see reason. She closed her eyes, as more tears spilt over her cheeks.

When she opened her eyes, Percy sat on his haunches, carved motionless in stone, watching her standing there, his letter in her hand, tears glistening in the cool light of the moon. He said nothing. He could say nothing. Hope was rising in him, in a breathless stranglehold.

Polly moved, shaking her head slightly as if clearing a haze. "Umm... I found your letter..." Percy watched her without moving. She stepped forward. "Percy?" She stopped. Just saying his name caused her mind to spin. "Percy, please... don't go." Fresh tears.

His shoulders melted as he bowed his head in his palm. "Oh, thank God," he whispered. He looked up and Polly was coming towards him, slowly as if she feared to tread. "Percy...

I…" She stopped and swallowed hard as she reached out and touched his shoulder.

"Polly?" He searched her eyes for the truth. And what he saw made his heart leap. She had finally seen him. Her eyes were open and clear… full of agonized tears but seeing. There was no veil of distance, just doubt and uncertainty. "Polly? I cannot stay…"

"But Percy… please…"

He silenced her objections with the tip of his finger. "Shhh. I mean I cannot stay like this any longer. I said in the letter my sickness has changed me. I am restless, I cannot be satisfied staying knowing that…"

"Oh Percy… you could come and go… just as before. I would try not to hold on to you too tightly. I promise… I will try!"

"But that is just it, Polly. It cannot be 'just like before'. That is what I mean: I cannot do *that* anymore." The reality of the statement hit Polly like a blow… and she crumpled, kneeling at his side. Percy lifted her chin and spoke gently. "Polly – listen to me. Listen. I *want* you to hold on to me. I want that more than anything. I love you. I want you to marry me. Polly please – will you marry me?"

"Marry you?"

Percy swallowed. Was it too much? Was it too great a distance for her to travel so quickly? He nodded. "Please. *This* time I am asking you."

She bowed her head drying her eyes quietly, as he waited. Relief flooded her being with warmth. Security wrapped her heart in a blanket. She smiled… safe… loved… desired. Happy mischief twinkled unseen in her damp eyes. "I don't know that I can. There's a problem…"

"Problem?" Percy's voice strained.

Polly sat up and swiped her tears. She looked him full in the face. "I don't have any dowry. I used to have a house… but this man – well, he took it…" She smiled cheekily… waiting for him to twig she was kidding with him.

But he didn't return her smile. She was obviously alluding to the return of the title-deed. He searched her eyes, looking for a sign as to why she would refuse accepting back the ownership of her house. He knew she was proud and independent; that's why he had intended her not to see the letter until tomorrow. It was absurd! In all seriousness he replied, "I understood the house was sold fair and square."

"Well, yes, I suppose so… but it remains that I have no dowry, just a debt to this man…" She paused and added as an afterthought. "He is a decent man though… honest, faithful, strong… quite handsome." Percy's shoulders relaxed. He knew then he was safe, and the dowry issue faded in the glory of the moment. Only love could speak of him like that.

"And you feel that being in debt to this 'decent man'… doesn't leave you free to marry me?"

"I just wondered what you thought about that… marrying a penniless, obligated widow, with no dowry."

"I don't recall asking for an inventory. I just asked you to marry me."

"But it is something ye should consid…"

"Just answer the question!"

"Yes."

"Really? Say it again…"

"Yes Percy. I would be honoured to be your wife."

* * *

When Percy finally retired, he found the deed to the house under the table where it had floated unseen. He picked it up and laid it on the table. Would it have changed anything… if she had seen it? Everything had changed for him: greys burst into colour! He smiled as he lay exhausted on his bunk, his energy sapped, his heart ablaze, and his mind praising God.

The next day Percy took a moment to shuffle Polly aside. "I was thinking… would it make a difference to ye… having dowry?"

"Percy! I was kidding!" She laughed at the twist on his mouth, and marvelled at feeling so young, so alive. "I thought dowry was only an issue for the groom to be. It is your decision to be encumbered with a debt-laden wife. If you're willing – I'm willing. This is actually a financially sound move for me…" she offered light-heartedly.

"That's crazy! You make it sound as if you plotted this all along. There never was a question of dowry – was there?"

She laughed again. She was enjoying seeing him try so hard. "Oh, I confess – it was all I could think of in that moment to extract just a little revenge… just a little. You have put me through so much agony," she finished sheepishly.

"Agony? Me girl, I'm thinking ye don't know the meaning of the word. You have driven me to distraction over and over!"

"Percy – you nearly died!" Polly flew back at him. The energy with which she said it made him stop and pause.

The rejection he felt during his sickness, momentarily forgotten, now rose again, fresh, and raw. "So, you noticed that, did ye?"

She felt the hurt in his question. She looked at him amazed. "For weeks I have noticed nothing else! What do you mean?" Percy looked at her and said nothing. "Percy – tell me. What did you mean?"

"I dreamt – I sensed – that you were there urging me to keep fighting. So, I did. But when I woke… I realised you were not there, and I waited. You never came. I nearly caved. It seemed too hard to push through again… for nothing. That is why I decided to leave."

"You never saw me?"

"The other girls were there. And I appreciate what they did… I really do, but Polly – I wanted you there. I needed *you*."

"But I *was* there… didn't you feel me sponge your fever? When you were passed danger, I came back in between working… the girls were getting so tired… and you slept so much… you were very sick. I was so scared."

He could not doubt the sincerity in her eyes. "So… it was true after all. I thought it must have been a dream."

Polly's eyes clouded. "Oh Percy, it was close… so close. We nearly missed each other altogether! I have been so angry that I could let that happen. I feel I have wasted such a lot of time."

Percy grabbed her hands, as she swung around agitated. He felt a perverse desire to agree with her wholeheartedly, but he checked himself, and kissed her gently instead. "And what would have happened before now? You know our God takes pleasure in perfect timing."

"So, I take it, the dowry is not really an issue for you... even though you bring it up again?" She regretted her ill-timed attempt at humour.

"Well… there was another page in the letter that I found under the table. I wasn't sure whether you didn't see it fall… or threw it away. You can choose whether you want it or not. It still stands."

Percy drew the self-scribed transfer of title deed from his pocket and handed it to her. He needed to know whether it made a difference. Perhaps she would see that she didn't need him after all. She read it without emotion, folded it and put it on the table. "Well, there goes my last vestige of excuse. I will certainly have to marry you now."

* * *

17.

Jane bubbled over with excitement at the news of her mother's betrothal, and the last thing she, or anyone else, wanted to do was to tackle insurmountable piles of someone else's laundry. Still, Miriam insisted it was important for the school to continue, and the extra funds might allow for little special treat or two with a wedding in the wings. So, Miriam marshalled the troupes together to attack the offending routines head on. She made Andi supervise reading exercises after lunch as if nothing out of the ordinary had happened at all. Percy attended to business that had slipped in his sickness, and when he was around, he came to share the evening meal with the family.

On such an evening he sat listening to the banter of girls, talking through their day as they worked their way around rich wallaby stew, laden with fresh vegetables and sided with thick slabs of bread. They talked and joked about their day. Jo shared with generous and graphic details, her most disgusting moment, while Andi gagged on a particularly lumpy piece of parsnip. Jane mentioned the large brown snake she'd seen along the creek again. Bridget commented that Mrs Thornton's sister-in-law's cousin had decided to go west – following some new-fangled idea that there were fortunes to be made beyond the impassable mountains to the west. Her eyes were alight with rumours that the Governor had refused further land grants to the Blaxland brothers, and they were determined to lead an exploration party to penetrate the ranges in search for additional pasture.

Percy absorbed that news with dread. He knew the brothers' reputation for self-promotion. He had no doubt that their pursuit of pastoral lands for their stock would eventually mean they'd discover ways to cross these impenetrable mountains. But what would they do with these new opportunities? How would they negotiate with those they met? Would the people who already lived there receive them? Percy knew the answers from experience... and it seemed to him that the cost of land could never be worth so high a price.

He shook his head at the bleak turn of his thoughts. Today he would not dwell on them. Today was a day for celebrating. He waited for a pause in the conversation, but there seemed no right moment to make his announcement. So, he just dropped it in. "Today I arranged for The Banns to be read," he casually remarked.

Polly stopped chewing and put down her fork. She looked at him. "You did? So soon?"

He thought this was part of the plan. "Don't we want a minister of religion to marry us?"

"Of course. But why now?" Polly looked at her stew. Would he ever talk to her first instead of just organising things?

"Because now is better than later." Percy was mystified. Did she have to question everything?

Jane looked from one face to the other. The light-hearted banter had dried up. She could feel the tension between them, and a tight knot of fear twisted in her stomach. Surely not! They loved each other. "Why do they have to read 'The Bands'?" she asked Andi quietly.

Andi had no idea what they were talking about, so she asked Jo with a shrug. "Do you know what Bands they have to read?"

Jo prodded Miriam. "What are *Bands* and why are we reading them?"

Miriam was shocked. For girls who knew so much, this seemed a strange omission in common knowledge. "*The Banns*? Don't you know?"

"Well, no – or I wouldn't be asking!" snapped Jo. Tension, however mild, is a contagious condition.

It was hard to explain. Miriam tried her best. "It's the notice given in church before a wedding. They read it out for three weeks before you can marry."

Andi looked at her puzzled. "Why?" She'd never heard of such a thing.

"So, you can get married in the church of course."

"Why can't you anyway?" persisted Jo. Miriam shrugged and went back to her private thoughts. As far as she was concerned, if that's what you had to do, you just did it. She waited for Polly to 'Return Thanks' to God for their meal and started to clear the table.

As Polly rose to help, Percy gently placed his hand on her wrist. "I'm sorry. I meant it as a surprise."

"Well, it was certainly that," said Polly shortly.

Percy took his hand away. "I thought this is what we wanted!"

Polly sat down again. "Percy – that's just it. You've been away. I'm dying to see you and catch up with everything that has happened around here, but instead of talking to me…

you're off organising my life. In case you didn't realise, I don't want you organising my life! I want to plan *our* life together. Just talk to me, okay? That's all."

"That's all? You're mad because I didn't talk to you about this?"

"What else? And I'm not angry!"

"Not because of the readings?"

"No, of course not! I couldn't be more pleased about that..." and she left Percy looking after her as if he had just discovered he was engaged to some extra-terrestrial alien that spoke a completely unknown language. Percy sighed and looked at Jane bewildered and shrugged. He smiled at the tight little expression on her face. "Your Mother is one of the most confounding creatures I have ever come across. You don't take after her, do you?" he said lightly – trying to make her serious eyes smile. "Two of you might be more than I can handle."

"Don't you love her?" Jane asked gravely.

"I do love her very much. Why would you doubt that?"

"Because you argue. My father argued all the time... he hurt us..."

Percy's jaw dropped in horror at the worries that crowded this little girls' heart. "Oh Janie! I love your mother, and you, very much.... *Very* much! I will never hurt you! I promise! I am sworn to protecting you and your mother. Jane, this is my life!"

"But... you shouldn't argue when you love someone!"

"But even when you love someone, you don't always agree or understand... but it's okay. We will get there. We will learn to talk things through. Your mother is right. I am used to doing things one way… and I have to learn to do them together now. It just might take some time. And I will need all the help I can get… and lots of love and lots of understanding." He paused. "Would you help me get better at this? Help us be a family and work together?" Jane nodded quietly. She felt a little better… but it still seemed that if you loved someone enough, there would be no disagreements. Percy saw her hesitation. "Who do you love most in the whole wide world?" he asked her.

"Mum…"

"Of course! And do you ever feel cross with her? Think that she doesn't understand you as well as she ought?"

Jane looked at him. "Well, I guess…"

"When?"

"I was scared of the snake today, but she says I still have to go down to the creek to do my chores…"

"Do you think your Mum still loves you… even though she doesn't quite understand how scary the snake is?"

"Yeah! Of course…"

"Jane – it's sort of the same when we're grown-up… we still need to explain what scares us… and listen to each other. Sometimes we get busy, or tired and forget. But it doesn't mean we don't love each other. Being a family is trying to help each other remember the important things… okay?"

"But my father…" her voice trailed off.

Percy cringed. *James Gartery – you have a lot to answer for*, he thought soberly. "There's a heap of things I don't understand Jane… big things and little things. Your father is one of the big things. We try to forgive and try to do better…"

"But he hurt Mum so bad!" A sob caught in her throat.

"And he hurt you too… and…" Percy could not finish speaking the thoughts that came. He closed his eyes momentarily to block out the images of hurt.

"So why should I forgive that? It isn't fair!" Jane's voice was high and tense.

Percy looked a little amazed at the depth of understanding a child could have. She was so right. It was not fair! "In the Bible Jesus asks us to forgive each other, because he knows holding onto the pain hurts us more…"

"How?" Tears glistened in her grey-green eyes; her light lashes clumping together with the moisture.

A lump gathered in Percy's throat. He also wanted forgiveness to come with permission to strangle the offender. That would feel so much better. "'*Forgive us our trespasses, as we forgive them that trespass against us.*' That's the way Jesus said it, so I guess that is the best line of attack. Forgiveness is doing the laundry of our soul. We need to be washing it out when it gets soiled… when we feel hateful or mean. It'd be pretty good if once you washed a shirt, you could wear without it ever getting dirty again."

Jane laughed at that. She certainly understood laundry. Imagine how much less washing there would be to do! Percy continued the thought. "Sometimes I think I've forgiven someone, and I've washed it all clean… and then I look around and it all seems dirty again… so I need to go back to Jesus – to clean me again."

"If he does that for everyone, he must have a really big scrubbing board!" said Janie with a grin.

Percy nodded and sensed that she understood; possibly a whole lot better than he did himself. She paused quietly with her eyes closed and her lips moved in a silent prayer. Then she looked up at Percy. She leaned over and wrapped her thin arms around his neck. "Thanks for coming Percy. I love you too." And she skipped out lightly, free from the shadowy burdens of the past.

* * *

Percy found Polly outside. She was leaning on the verandah-post gazing at the changing colours of the setting sky. He stood there for a while before she spoke. She had heard every word of his conversation with Jane, and it tugged mightily on her heart. "Percy, this is new for me too. I have been struggling so long to be well, that I don't want to lose ground. I appreciate the space you give me – just to be me… even though I find it terrifying at times. I know what you have given me is an enormous gift. Thank you."

Percy let the words soak into his soul. Being together was not about being perfect but allowing someone else to care back. No one ever said that was easy. He shifted his feet restlessly as he remembered why he had sought her out. "Polly I was wondering if you would come with me to the church tomorrow – even though it is as plain as the nose on your face that I am organising your life again."

Polly hesitated. The church was intimidating. They were not welcome to worship there, and the clergy had a harsh, uncompromising reputation. Still, it was their choice to be married in a church before God, so if Percy was with her, it would be all right. "Thanks for asking me – and not telling me what to do instead." She reached out and stroked his cheek. "There has not been a lot of that in my life. Do you know how amazing it is to have a man that I can have a rational disagreement with?"

Percy suddenly was overcome with a bout of coughing. Rational was the last thing he'd call it! "Sorry…" he said between spasms, "I seem to have something stuck in my throat!"

Polly grinned and playfully hit his back between the shoulder blades. "Can I get you anything for your cough? A compress of nettles for your chest? A linctus of warm ginger and lemon for your throat? I didn't think so. You are suddenly better!" She laughed. "I would love to accompany you on such an excursion. I guess we need to undergo the inspection of approval."

"The Curate wants to see our pardons before he reads *The Banns*. I thought we would go and present them tomorrow. Then it will be done."

Polly quickly withdrew her hand as if a snake had bitten it. She started to shake, and her breaths came in short, sharp gasps. Percy quickly grabbed her as she collapsed totally into his arms.

* * *

Polly lay on her bed with the collar of her blouse loosened. Miriam lent over her wiping her forehead with a cool cloth. Percy paced outside the room like lion. "Whatever is wrong?" he searched in his mind for a clue as to what might trigger her hysterical collapse. The episode seemed completely beyond explanation. The curate was a man recently arrived from Kent. She could not possibly know him. Was the idea of finalising the details that made their marriage a certainty, too much? Was she still so afraid – that deep down she couldn't bear the idea of it at all? His thoughts went around and around as he paced up and down.

Andi slipped into the room with a cup of warm tea, and Percy could see through the door Polly lying in bed propped up against pillows. Her face was pale and drawn. Suddenly she seemed very sick and frail. His heart exploded in protective compassion. Would things ever be normal for them? Would they always have to hedge around ghouls and ghosts from the past?

The confines of the small house and his inability to be ushered into the intimacy of his betrothed's bedroom propelled him outside. *"Oh God!"* he yelled silently to the stars. *"Ten minutes ago, we were sharing a comfortable moment and making progress!"* He was trying so hard to learn this new way of living. He didn't want to be the dictators that he saw many of his peers were within their marriages. But sometimes… oh it would be easier, just to shake her into compliance… and yell at her to be better! "Oh God!" he screamed again. He struck out and his fist hit the rough trunk of a bloodwood tree that stood unmoved by the ranting in his mind. "God, this is so unfair!" and he weakly leant his forehead against the hard, ribbed bark, stained with dark red sap that bled from thick sticky wounds. It mirrored the bleeding wounds inflicted on his heart.

How long he was there he was not sure but slowly he became aware of Jo and Andi. They stood back waiting for him to acknowledge their presence. He turned to them. They stood close together holding a lantern. They said nothing.

"How is she?" he asked, almost inaudibly.

"She's sitting up. She doesn't remember falling." Andi answered the questions quietly.

"Is she okay?"

"She's had a drink of tea. I think so…"

"Did she say what was wrong?"

"Sort of."

"What do you mean – 'sort of'?" Andi looked at Jo and Jo looked at the ground and scuffed her boots. They didn't respond. Percy's heart skipped a beat and started to feel hollow all over again. "Don't beat around the bush… just give it to me square. What did she say was wrong?"

The girls looked at each other again. Andi eventually nodded and Jo took a deep breath. "Percy… she says she can't marry you." There – it was out. They waited for the eruption. But it didn't come.

He looked at them… waiting. "What else?"

"What else? Isn't that enough?" said Jo incredulously.

"Well, why?"

"We don't know. She won't say. She said…" How could they explain the incoherent jumble that had tumbled out of her mouth?

"What?" Percy's voice was flat.

"She said… we're not sure. Percy, she's not making sense. One minute she's in the past and she's still a convict, and she says she can't burden you… but in the next breath she says she's done her time and is free. But then she mutters that her life is destroyed... burnt to ashes... she keeps saying that... *'burnt to ashes'*. We don't get it... she's just totally overwhelmed."

"She said she didn't want to burden me?"

They nodded silently.

"You think she still loves me?"

"Yeah, of course."

"Well, I'll have to see her."

"You can't... she won't let us... we tried."

"Can't?" Percy's voice rose in challenge. "Be blowed I can't!"

Andi quickly tried to pour oil on these troubled waters. Percy had been taking it so well, but before she could speak, he burst past them into the house. He stormed into her room defying all protocol of decency. "Where is it?" he demanded. "You don't want me organising your life! But fair go Polly I have tried tiptoeing around! Just tell me where your Pardon is and I will go to the curate myself and then we are getting married even if I have to carry you there!"

Polly blinked at him. Sadness welled up in an aura of hopelessness. When she spoke, her voice was remarkably calm. "I don't have it, Percy. James... said... well, I thought it would help if he really understood I was free. He despised me being a convict. When I showed him – he burnt it. It was burnt to ashes..." She closed her eyes as the flames freshly burnt at her heart. "I saw it burn. It's gone. If I tell them I don't have it – I will be recalled. If I don't present the paper, we can't be married." Tears spilt over onto the bed covers in anguish.

"Percy. I've done my time. I can't go back there. I'm sorry – but I cannot marry you."

"Well, we won't go to the church then. We'll just be married by ourselves: before God. He'll understand."

Polly's voice was resigned. "No Percy. No. I'm sorry. I really am," and then she closed her tear washed eyes and rolled over. For the yet another time in his life Percy was shut out.

* * *

18.

Percy poked at his campfire with a stick. He pushed the red, hot coals around. Images of Polly's pardon, burning and curling under the heat, tormented him. Rage enveloped his senses. He sat frustrated and weak with hopeless fury at the site of Burilda's murder. Tangible hate pulsated the air. He had destroyed both his loves! *The sea was too good for him!* Percy had his opportunity, and he had let it pass him by! For the first time, Percy regretted his decision to walk away from the cry for blood. He regretted his decision to walk the way of Jesus instead. He regretted his patience and his long suffering. What did it bring? Just more suffering, and that was the truth!

He stabbed the coals again. Heat and light flared, and he jumped as he spotted three figures out of the corner of his eye – white and ethereal. He turned startled, to see Jane standing in a long cotton nightdress, Jo and Andi close beside her. "What the dickens are you doin' here?" He glared at them angrily. "Go back to your mother! She needs you."

Andi quietly took Jane's hand. "I told you sweetheart… let's go."

Jane pulled her hand away and didn't move. She glared at Percy long and hard. He stared back. Eventually she walked closer and stood over him, her long straight hair glowed in the firelight. Her little frame looked almost angelic. "You're a liar," she accused matter-of-factly. Whatever tirade Percy expected, it was not that. The blow hit him, and he physically recoiled.

She didn't move. She stood there. Percy closed his eye to avoid looking at her. Dear Jane. He could have better stood up under the scorn of Polly herself. When he spoke, his voice was softer. "Jane, go home. It's late and cold…"

"No! I will not! I promised."

"Promised what?"

"You asked me to help… if you forgot. And I promised, so I have to help you remember."

Percy groaned. The tension in his heart was strangling him: the struggle to hate one, and love another, warred in a brutal battle. "I didn't forget anything," he said sullenly. All he could do was remember. He wished he could forget.

"Then you're just a liar!"

"About what?" He thought he already knew.

"About how to forgive. You have to go back to the washboard. You have to!" He hadn't expected that. He winced in pain. The shock took his breath away as he stared at the fire. He tried to conjure up the images of forgiveness that were once given to him in the coals, but they remained dazzling orange-hot, frozen, and still.

He got up and walked away into the shadows. Every word of the conversation he had with Jane followed him and taunted his ears. He had said those things with sincerity. He had thought he earned authority to speak because he walked that way with experience. But now, every excuse, every reason, every evasion possible, sprang to his mind. Such a short time ago… but oh, how he had underestimated the magnetism, the pleasurable appeal of hatred. There was a distinct comfort in the alluring embrace of malice. Its bitter grip was too strong, and he could not disentangle himself from its devious tentacle hold.

He looked over at Andi and Jo standing in the shadows. But instead of looking defiant, they had their eyes closed. They held on tightly to each other in solidarity as they simply tried to surround this minefield of emotion with their protective prayers. Had he expected judgement from them because his own body oozed condemnation from every pore? He looked away quickly and his gaze collided with Jane's open, trusting, disappointed eyes.

"You expect me to do this, don't you?" he said amazed. She simply nodded. "Why? There is no justice!" he yelled at her. It was an unfair thing to thrust at a child, but fair was not Percy's game. When he saw her wince, his heart softened. "Oh Jane! How can you be bothered with me?"

Jane didn't move. Only her eyes followed his angry pacing back and forth. "We love you, Percy. Mum misses you so much."

"Jane – you don't understand. We can't be married now."

"It's okay. God will make a way where there is no way." She had heard her mother say it so many times that it came as naturally as breathing. Percy stopped pacing and looked at her. *"Come as a little child…"* It was so effortless for her to have such faith. Logically… it was foolishness, but faith defies logic.

He turned then and walked towards her. She did not move or back up. Percy squatted on his haunches in front of her and took her hands. "You're not scared of me?" he said amazed.

She smiled at him. "You promised not to hurt us. I don't think you would lie about *that*." A tear fell from Percy's clear eye, and Jane reached up and wiped it with the frilled cuff of her sleeve. Percy looked at her sadly. If only she knew how close he had come to throwing unforgivable pain her way. He had scared himself. He was no better than the man he despised.

"You know something? I miss you too. You are right – I need to do some business with the Master Launderer. Jane, go home. Tell your Mum I will be there in the morning. We will find God's way through the wilderness."

* * *

What is released when a heart humbles itself? In the morning, Percy braced himself with the protection of God. He didn't know if he could do this. How could he be part of their lives, but not be able to live in the fullness of it? "God – you know I can't do it without you. Perhaps I started to think that I could – that I had got far enough along to be strong by myself. Well," he conceded, "the truth is I need you more than ever!"

He walked along, passing a small contingent of soldiers on their way from the barracks; their red jackets and white crosses marching regimentally, their tall black hats bobbing in rhythm. One careless word could expose Polly's vulnerable position and have her sent back to the convict work-gangs under the hands of these soldiers. That thought sobered his step.

No pardon? It seemed impossible. How she had celebrated holding the evidence of her freedom in her hand! He remembered her reserved delight and compulsion to share her liberation with someone, anyone! Sadly, the passing possum trapper with smelly pelts and a deformed face was the only audience for such a momentous event. Who would have thought, Percy mused, that the same man was returning to grieve the theft of that freedom? She had so carefully, reverently smoothed it out on the table. Percy remembered feeling an unaccountable fear stab at his insides. "Polly Gartery," he had said, "take this and find a safe place. Treasure it like your mother's emerald heirloom. Don't give anyone the opportunity to steal this away. This is your inheritance now – your freedom to pass on to Jane."

She looked at him stunned, and he left quickly. He didn't want to confess he had overheard her responding to Jane's pleas to tell her about something of her life in England. Polly could only think of the rich green fields of the estate where she grew up... reflecting the deep green of the heirloom necklace that was to be given on her twenty-first birthday. It represented everything that was so different from the harsh, dry browns of the Australian summer. She never received that emerald necklace, and now over a decade later, and half a world away, it seemed so vain that it ever captured the imagination of her heart. The dreams she dreamed now were much more valuable than emerald stones set in gold.

"Oh God," Percy prayed, "where is the exchange? Where is the joy for mourning? Where is the beauty for ashes? Show me how you can bring beauty out of so many ashes. I'm not seeing it here!"

Afterward Percy could not account for it. A picture rose up before his eyes. He saw himself crouching by the hearth fire, picking up a charred piece of paper. Then he was mechanically clearing away the chaotic remains in the house – replacing a hidden security box in the wall. They were disjointed images of the broken debris of his life and Polly's shattered world, joined together. But it was not a memory he actually remembered living.

He was so stunned by the revelation that a passer-by collided into his back, taken unaware by his sudden halt. The man protested with curses, "tactless, vulgar barbarians in this god-forsaken cess-pool!" Percy stood for a moment oblivious to his outburst. Then he shoved him out of the way, sending forth another tirade of obscenities. He ran, urgency tearing at his lungs.

He burst into the main room with such sudden ferocity that Polly, sitting by the window in her chair quietly praying for Percy's arrival, started to her feet in shock. He brushed passed her and heaved the sideboard aside and clumsily felt for the hidden draw. Frustration clawing at his face as his rough calloused fingers unsuccessfully mauled the wall. "Polly! Where is it? The box – where is it? I know it's here. Show me!"

Shock and pain were nakedly visible in every crease of Polly's face. "It's not there Percy. I told you the truth – I did! Please don't make me prove my word. Please…"

He paused, breathing heavily, every fibre in his body shaking. He dropped his chin to his chest and breathed in a prayer of restraint. "Polly – you're a good woman. I ain't disbelieving you, but I am needing ye to allow me this. Trust me – like you are wanting me to trust you. Please. I'm asking where the drawer is."

He stepped aside, tension pounding in his chest. Was it true… or was it another wistful imagination – born out of numbing grief, shrouded in shadows of trauma? He could not be sure until he saw for himself.

Polly searched his face and quietly knelt. Tears sprang to her eyes as she automatically felt for the notch and worked out the box with long trembling fingers. Percy gently put his hand on her shoulder, and he felt her wince. She closed her eyes as the drawer scrapped out, dust from the mud wall showering her wrist. Polly removed the lid and handed him the open tray, but he didn't take it from her hand. She just heard him whisper, "Oh God. It was true." Gently he cradled the scarred document retrieved from its hidden haven. He was sure that enough remained legible to be issued with a replacement.

* * *

19.

The girls gathered outside the little church waiting for Polly and Percy to emerge. "What sort of wedding is that!" said Jo with disgust as they hung around outside feeling about as welcome as fleas on a dog. "It's not a real wedding without lots of people, and a party and something special. It's just wrong!" Even little Jane missed out because the curate dogmatically declared he wasn't going to make a carnal spectacle out of the sanctity of matrimony.

"Narrow-minded nitwit!" declared Andi when Polly had told them what to expect. "The whole point is to make a spectacle of it. Be blowed if we're going miss out because of his sanctimonious rules! Even Jesus went to a wedding reception and had a party!"

Polly was disappointed for them, but she had no desire to take on the church. The goal was to get the certificate, and to do that, they needed to play by the rules. It was more precious since they nearly were not able to.

But despite their objections, they all waited meekly outside the church. Not even Miriam was ushered into the inner sanctuary even though she was over twenty-one, literate and a family friend. They required a *man* to witness the event. In the end they called a nameless worker in from the garden who made an unintelligible mark beside their names. It was Percy who suggested they celebrate their wedding together with the special treats that Andi had devised, by going on a bush retreat. When they came back, they would settle into their everyday routines as kin.

Miriam decided right from the start she would stay behind and supervise the school, rather than suspend classes when things were going well. A holiday was never a thing Bridget would pass up, but Miriam did some serious talking about family bonding, and Bridget relented in letting the girls go along without her. Once Andi found out their plans, she felt they were intruding on the honeymooners too. But she knew Jane would need some time with her newlywed 'parents' and Jo agreed they should keep her company and shuffle her off at every opportunity to allow the couple some time alone.

* * *

So it was, that they stood in a small, fern covered glen, a canopy of trees overhead for their celebration. Wild magenta lilly-pilly berries decorated their bush chapel like confetti in one of natures' glorious displays. They had seen a little bowerbird not far from here. It felt like they were decorating their own little love bower, with all the curious things the bush could offer as adornments. The girls braided each other's hair and entwined tiny white gumnut flowers in between the twists of Polly's auburn hair. Jane had collected a tiny posy of bush leaves and gumnuts and was solemnly standing beside her mother. The clear icy tinkle of bellbird chimes rang and echoed through the trees. "Wedding bells," whispered Andi. No detail had been overlooked in this bush ceremony.

Percy stood holding Polly's hand. He turned and looked deep into her eyes. "It is right to celebrate our wedding here in the bush… not because I was Aborigine… but because this is where I found God, myself, and my family. Oh yes, The Tribe accepted me and taught me much, but I don't have the roots that they have. Polly, we need to put down our own roots. They know their unique place of belonging, their own Dreaming… now we have to find our own. This country is full of precious dreams, beautiful and fertile like the green of an emerald. Polly this is our inheritance to pass on to Jane. There is much we have lost and grieve, but that is not the sum of it all, because God has given us today… to start a future!"

Polly smiled and blinked her thick red lashes. That he alluded to her necklace – and even now she always thought of it as "her" necklace – it made her think he regretted having no family treasures to give her. "Percy, there is richness right here. Being able to anticipate our future, no jewels can match this. Don't let us forget how to dream."

"Forget? This is a land of dreams! Even though we never wanted or intended to be here, it is like we have been transplanted. We have become part of fulfilling the destiny of this place – for the generations to come…" He paused then because Andi burst into tears. She was so moved that he was pleading faithfulness to all those nameless future generations who would follow. Her own family was part of that future - including her grandmother, her parents, even herself… and he didn't even know.

Percy looked deep into Polly's eyes. "Polly as your husband, I pledge myself to this end. I will help make this land become a place where our children will be free to dream and know that it is possible to see those things fulfilled."

Andi held a crumpled a handkerchief in her hand and blew her nose loudly. "That," she sniffed, "is the most romantic thing I have ever heard!"

Jo quietly took Jane's hand and whispered in her ear. "I think they need a quiet moment by themselves. It's all getting a bit mushy." She grabbed Andi's hand also and pulled her away. "Get a grip Andi..." she whispered, "This is not a movie... They need their space."

"But Jo... they might say something more!"

"Exactly – so let's give them some time alone..." She pushed Andi out of the way. They followed a little gully down to the creek, clear and crystal as it tumbled over rocks. They stayed there, floating leaves, building rock walls, and playing with Jane.

Polly was barely aware they had gone; she reached up and touched Percy's cheek. "My turn..." she whispered. "Percy, as your wife, I want to be your soul mate, your friend, your confidant. I want to be able to share your dreams... and trust you with mine. I pledge myself to you... body, soul and spirit."

Then she did something she had desired to do since that moonlight night when they had found each other again. She reached up and loosened his eye patch, so that it fell to the side. He looked at her quizzically and instinctively turned his scarred, deformed side away. She held his firm chin and gently moved it back, so she was looking full into his face. "Percy you are not ugly to me. I have never known love such as you have given me... that is so fine. Still wear your patch – I know you have your reasons... but I want you to know that I love you. I love your battle scars. I want you to be able to wear them proudly around me, my love. I have scars too... and they have made me who I am. In a way, they have brought us together.

That is something I will never regret... or feel ashamed of. I want you to know that." She went to retie the string, but before she could, he gathered her in his arms and kissed her, long and lingering, as a husband kisses his bride.

* * *

20.

When Percy and Polly followed the girls' trail to the creek, evening was coming on. It was cool and the water in the creek gurgled its gentle song over the shallow rocks that lined the edge of deeper water holes. Andi sat on a large rock hugging Jane, quietly watching the water, and Jo was pointing wordlessly to the round concentric ripples in the stillness of the clear pool where they sat. A platypus and its mate playfully tumbled over each other innocently unaware of their enraptured audience. Their wide flat tails, sleek brown backs and rubbery bills flipped up above the water's surface sending out more ripples that found their way to the edge of the bank.

Jane suddenly sneezed and the furry couple did one final flip and disappeared into the shadowy depths of the water by the bank. The girls sat there for a moment unwilling to break the sacred hush that surrounded them. Jo wanted to hold on to this feeling forever but on the other hand she wanted to jump to her feet and yell excitedly to the world: "Wow! Did you see that?" In the end she just sighed... long, happy and contented.

Jane sniffled, and Polly wrapped a shawl around her shoulders. "You'd better come back to the fire... it's getting cool." Andi watched Polly and Jane walk on together and a sad feeling washed over her. She missed her Mum – her real home. These people had surrounded her like another family. They were her friends... and how she wished she could have both. She knew it was not possible. If she had to choose – she would go home.

Percy led the way back to their small fire, where he had some superb bush tucker roasting in the coals. The girls ate and stretched themselves out contentedly beside the fire. "Sorry girls... you can't camp here tonight." Percy was very definite. They looked over to see him standing by a bush bridal gunya freshly made, decorated with boughs of gumnut flowers and grevilleas. "There is a special guest room in a local tree that would be more sheltered..."

"I get it... more private," muttered Jo who rolled over, quite reluctant to disturb herself.

"You've stayed there before."

"Come on Jo," said Andi... "I'm tired and they want some privacy... you're the one who insisted on space if I remember correctly." Andi ignored her protests and pulled her to her feet.

On the edge of the camp was a tree: the tree. It stood tall and majestic, the hollow base, opening like a door. Andi looked shocked as she remembered their flight in the storm. "It looks kinda different now... not scary at all."

"Looks like a bedroom to me," said Jo "I'm dog-tired."

"You have to work so hard in this place to do everything, even to have a holiday. I reckon I could sleep standing on a log."

"As long as I have my trackies and T-shirt. Glad we brought them." She folded her skirts as a pillow and settled themselves, each wrapped in a swag blanket. Jane lay down between them coughing and sniffing and wriggling. She groaned and muttered, "I don't feel good...want to go and sleep with Mum."

Jo looked at Andi in the dim light of a lantern that fought vainly against the shadows in the tree. "Come on Janie... a good sleep might make all the difference. I think your Mum and Percy just want some alone time now."

Andi reached out and gave Jane a cuddle. She felt hot and squirmed uncomfortably. "Here, let's practice some writing until you can snuggle down and sleep..."

By the dim yellow light of the lamp, they carved their names into the side of the tree wall trying to distract her. But even that was soon abandoned. "I can't write anymore," whinged Jane uncooperatively. Andi stroked her hair and she eventually surrendered to a restless and uncomfortable sleep.

"Jo?" murmured Andi sleepily as she finally heard Jane's regular snuffled breathing. "I think that Polly and Percy make the perfect couple. Wouldn't it be weird if they were our ancestors?"

Jo barely heard her... she just grunted sleepily, and said, "I guess we'll never know... but you can bet they have influenced what Australia will become. Just now, that is the... best... promise... to make..." and she surrendered to the heavy embrace of sleep that churned about her.

Andi's only response was quiet regular breathing. Somewhere her lesson carved into the tree petered out and a dream began: Bridget and Mims stood in their practical serge pinafores and aprons in front of a modern classroom whiteboard in the new library at school. Classmates giggled without mercy at their funny clothes and clumsy handwriting. They were trying to spell "preposition". Andi watched as one of the girls, slowly emptied the middle out of her pen and blew a tight little spit-ball aimed straight at Bridget. It hit like a bullet on her face. Rapidly it got ugly. Bridget ducked and screamed as another boy joined in target practice. Her bright eyes flashed, and she flew around in a rage grabbing another kid who began pelting hard wads of rolled up paper. The perpetrator howled loudly as Miriam's strong work-toughened arms lifted him effortlessly out of his seat like a weighty bundle of laundry. Another came to his rescue. It was an all-out brawl. The class began banging their fists against their desks and scrapping their chairs angrily at these strange non-conforming students. Andi looked powerlessly at the door waiting for the teacher. Suddenly she realised *she* was the teacher. A blast of cold air blew their assignment papers around and around the room. "Stop it!" yelled Andi in angry frustration… "Stop it – they are my friends! They have as much right to be here as you! More! Heaps more… because they want it more than you do! Leave them alone! Leave them alone!"

"Andi! Andi – wake up! Andi!"

Jo's voice pierced her dream and she groggily tried to focus. "Jo – stop them…" she said breathing hard. The images still vividly held her mind.

"It's a dream Andi… it's okay…" The last of her sentence was muffled as thunder rumbled around the forest. Lightening flashed and a blast of cold air swirled up the leaf litter in their little wooden bedroom.

Andi was shaking and her hands felt sweaty. "Jo? I was in the library at school…"

"I'm here." Jo reached out and held her friend's hand. "Jane's taken the lamp and gone… over to her Mum no doubt... it's raining, but not as bad as that other storm. Still no point going out there now." Lightening forked and an enormous bang cracked the air. Flashes of light showed a steady fall of rain outside. They huddled together to keep warm.

"Jo, I actually think I've had enough 'back-to-nature' moments lately!"

"Got to admit... the platypus moment was so worth it!"

"True. I could do that again."

They good-naturedly bantered back and forth, trying to dispel the darkness of the inky night from penetrating into fear. They were safe... they were dry... they just had to wait until morning. Andi shifted her weight, and tried to stretch her cramped legs. "If I ever winge about my inner-spring mattress and doona again, please hit me. I promise to be forever content." She felt around and sifted some sticks out from under her. "Oh..."

Jo heard her voice change. "What?"

"I think I found our torch..."

"Really?"

Andi flicked it on and shone it around. The rain had subsided and already the grey of morning was lightening the shapes of the trees outside. Breakfast would still be ages away. She flicked off the torch. They nestled back down with every intention of dozing off. Some birds sang their first tentative morning calls. "Jo! Andi! Cooee!

Jo rolled over and groaned. "Married life must suit him... that's early even for Percy. Bet he expects us to find dry wood after the rain."

"Unless Jane's sick…" Andi said concerned. "She did seem a bit unwell."

The urgent calls came again. They struggled out of their bedroom, their trackpants dragging in the fresh mud. "Yeah! What's wrong?" she called out.

"Here! Here!" called his deep voice. "I found them! Over here!"

"But we're…"

Suddenly Scott, Ranger Dave and Mr Hollis surrounded them. "Oh, thank God! You are safe!" The relief in their voices was thick with emotion. They hugged them, and Ranger Dave threw a thick army style blanket over their shoulders.

The girls stood dazed as they struggled to register the monumental time shift that had taken place. Jo wrapped the blanket tightly around her. She felt strangely exposed standing there in her trackpants and T-shirt. "Yeah… we're… okay."

Andi remain motionless, shocked. "We never got to say goodbye." A tear rolled down her cheek. "I just wanted to let them know we are okay."

Mr Hollis carefully draped his arm around her shoulder. "I know sweet. It's been a long night. You just need to come back to camp. We've phoned your folks and they're coming to pick you up early. Sausages for breakfast. Reckon you could eat a horse."

"Just a sec… we left our torch…" Jo grabbed Andi's hand and they ducked back inside their refuge tree. Jo clicked on the light and shone it around inside the tree. "I just wanted to see… yes – there." On the wall of the trunk, surviving scars from bush fires and years of smoky campers was chiselled a large heart. In the middle of the heart was carved their names: 'Jo + Andi + Jane'.

Jo traced it with her finger. "See, she was okay Andi. Jane finished it. She was always our friend."

"Oh look…" Andi directed the light of the torch around the heart. "*Dreams do come true*," she read quietly. "Oh Jo. They really do."

"Ah huh," agreed Jo. "See this here…" She pointed the torch and started to read the names carved around the heart. Percival + Polly; Bridget + Thomas; Miriam + Serl; Jane + Ralph; Harriet + Bert…

"Jane made this tree her Dream Diary. These are her notes of those she loved. She came back to remind herself." Andi was struggling. "We will never know the stories of how their dreams came to be."

"Does it make them any less true? Just because we don't know?"

"We just can't pretend it never happened!" That was an affront to their memory, and how they had loved and looked after them.

"No, I guess not. But who would understand?" said Jo logically.

"We do…" Perhaps Andi needed to find her own Dream Diary. A place to help her remember her dreams as they come to be. That idea comforted her some.

"Girls… the camp has been up all night. We need to get back and let them know you're okay… and call off the search."

"Search?" That brought them out.

They were bundled off through the bush. The track was not far and before they could blink – kids, and leaders and Mrs Hollis surrounded them.

* * *

Josie, Sarah, Abby, and Lauren linked arms and encased them in a tight little circle. Lauren shouted, "One, two, three!" Together the girls began to chant: "We're a lean, mean, green camping machine!" Jo and Andi saw the relief and excitement on their faces and joined in. "Don't be seen without the green! We're the team! Wear the green! Yaaaaaah!"

The Green Girls fell all over them in an exuberant display of thankfulness, anxious to show how relieved they were. They pulled at their army blankets, to get in one extra hug. Andi stepped back and shrugged apologetically.

"It's okay girls…" Mrs Hollis laughed, "They've had a really big night. They may need some space…" And she shooed away the kids and sat them on a log. She placed an enamel plate of sausages, and bacon, and buttered toast in their laps. "Eat up girls. It takes a mighty appetite to stay out all night. Praise God, you are safe."

Never had charred sausages tasted so good. Jo looked at the manicured lawns of the park, the planted native gardens around the amenities block and the barbeques. She couldn't decide what she thought of 'progress' just now. The area was certainly beautiful, but it wasn't like it had been. She looked up and saw an eagle, circling on the currents high above the trees. Mrs Hollis came and sat beside them and followed their gaze. "I've heard the indigenous elders say that the eagle is the spiritual eyes of the bush. It allows them to see tucker that the hunters would have no natural way of knowing is there… and that is life-giving information for them…"

"Yeah, I've heard that too."

"I'm glad God's eyes are like that. He was looking out for you girls… and caring for you. He showed us where you were. We had no natural way of knowing. I'll think of that every time I see an eagle now."

Andi looked thoughtful and then said, "Do you know what I think of when I see an eagle? Dreams. Precious dreams! I want my dreams to have wings like that eagle, so that I can soar on them to amazing heights. I think that is what I learnt while I was away. To let my dreams have wings."

"So, what is your dream Andi? What bold thing will you breathe life into and give wings to?" asked Mrs Hollis quietly. They obviously had done a lot of thinking during their night-long ordeal.

Andi did not hesitate. "I want to teach – English and History. I want to do it so well that it comes alive!"

Jo looked at Andi and nodded. She understood. Then she looked back at the eagle, soaring effortlessly, its huge wing feathers dipping and ruffling as the air currents rushed over them. She watched the eagle's large wings circle around and around, getting smaller and smaller.

Jo bent down a picked up a gumnut off the ground. She rolled it over in her hand. It was one thing to have a dream, it was another thing to have the courage to make it happen. She wondered if she understood courage like that. Jo thought of Mims, Bridget and Jane, Polly and Percy. Each one in some way had shown extraordinary courage to keep going… to see their dreams be activated. *Thank you for sharing your dreams with me*, she whispered to them across the pages of history. *I think your dreams were precious... like the emeralds in your necklace Polly. You did look after them... you have given us a beautiful inheritance. Every dream you kept for us is a precious gem. We are so rich because you treasured them!*

More Books by this Author
Stand-alone Stories

Matt's Boys of Wattle Creek

When Matthew Lawson's three sons were born, he wrote each of them a letter outlining his hopes and prayers for their futures. When he decided to give up his city job and move to the little town of Wattle Creek, he could never have imagined the effect it would have on his young family. As Matt's boys grow to maturity and find their places in their community, will his dreams and prayers come to fulfilment? Will his boys develop their own faith in the eternal God? And will they each find the kind of love that Matt holds for his beautiful Josie?

Maggie & Minotaur

"For Maggie, the mythical Minotaur represented Romance – half man, half beast. The Minotaur was a monster created from centuries of classical Greek mythology and no normal man could withstand its strength...... Sooner or later she would accept that Theseus, the hero, did not exist. She knew that she would have to battle through the maze of reality and confront it herself...." Maggie Wick was shipped off to the city and high society life at the age of 12, where she would learn the ways of the rich and marry into a family of influence. What could have caused her sudden return to Henderson's Gap? Can she really settle back into life on the station, with all its diversity and challenges? Will she find fulfilment in her role as provisional schoolteacher? Will she ever figure out the "Captain", the mysterious, intimidating, station manager? When war comes to her little haven and Maggie's world comes crashing down, taking her loved ones and the captain with it, Maggie needs to find a way to survive. Will her faith be enough to protect her, and what of the Captain? Could he really be the Theseus who would do battle with her Minotaur?

#1 The Beachside Cottage

In this offering from Olwyn Harris, we meet the heartbroken and downtrodden Eliza-Beth Perkins. Eliza-Beth is facing the dire consequences of her choices and the possibility of life in the poorhouse. Then she, literally, runs into Jensen Harker. Jensen is facing his own heartbreak at the death of his wife and wants nothing more than to be left alone. But something in Eliza-Beth stirs him to make a rash proposal, thus rescuing her from her predicament. As we follow their journey together, will we see them find the healing they both desperately need?

#2 Petrea Downs

In the 2nd book in this series, we meet Meg. Meg's life has been turned upside-down, with her husband gone, trying to run Petrea Downs by herself, and disaster after disaster at every turn. Thankfully, her neighbour Everett Grossman is always there to help. The final blow comes when a cattle duffer tries to steal her only source of income, gets shot, and has to be nursed back to health in her living room. But, is Ben Harker really the villain he seems? And is Everett really the hero he makes himself out to be?

#3 The Writer's Retreat

The third book in the Homes of Healing trilogy introduces us to Tess, a romance writer, who prides herself on letting her characters tell their own story. When she arrives at Rocky Creek B&B, the run-down stone cottage looks like the perfect place for her to retreat to, not only to write her book, but to escape her past. Join her as she discovers her characters and explores their stories, and finds that God is intent on becoming part of her own story at the same time. As her relationship with the local publican challenges her to stop running, she realises that real life and real love can be messy and complicated. Can she honestly confront the ugly aspects in her own story, so that God can bring them both to a place of healing?

#1 Sapphires of Hope

"There is no way," she thought, "that I am going to use this!" She had desperately searched their cupboards for something, anything that would come close to what she needed for her catering project. She found only this old dilapidated breadbasket that looked like the sort of junk that comes from one of those tacky jumble-sale stalls..." Andi and Jo are best friends... they do pretty much everything together. So, when Andi has a catering assignment due, and only a tacky old basket to use, Jo helps her pull off the faded decorations, revealing a time-capsule of historical information, and in order to understand what it means, Andi and Jo ask their elderly neighbour to take them to visit the farm where the basket came from. They find themselves dumped back in history at the time of Federation, embroiled in circumstances that nearly cost Andi her life and threatens the livelihood of the people living there. How can they ever hope to keep going when things are spinning out of control?

#2 Rubies of Ambition

In the 2nd book in the Gem of Australia series, we again travel with Andi and Jo back in time. On this adventure, they meet the very beautiful and ambitious actress, Lillian Browning, who is on the run from the federal police. Andi and Jo accompany her back to her hometown, where they find she is not well received. Will Lillian find a balance between the past that calls her and the ambitions that drive her?

#1: A Spacious Place

In this first instalment of the Guthrie's Lot series, set in the late 1800s, we meet Irvin Guthrie, a practical, no-nonsense man with a sick wife and a small child to care for. When his wife's doctor suggests they move to a warmer climate, he spends everything he has on a property that ends up not being what he expected.

Joanna Grenham has dreams of being a schoolteacher. When an opportunity presents itself, she jumps at the chance, only to find herself given no choice but to care for Irvin's sick wife and child.

Will Irvin and Joanna make the most of their circumstances, or will they forever find life as hard and unyielding as the ground in A Spacious Place?

#2: A Level Path

In the second instalment of the Guthrie's Lot series, it is now the late 1960s. Here we meet Irvin's granddaughter Iris. Iris hungers for excitement and adventure, and she won't find that in Gumleigh, or with the ever-predictable Dave. The last thing she expected was for Dave to follow her across the world to England as she tries to find direction and meaning.

Will Iris finally see through the charismatic, but ultimately selfish, Stan, or will Dave leave England alone and leave Iris to find her own way to A Level Path?

#3: The Crying Tree

In this final episode of the Guthrie's Lot series, the year is now 2010. We meet Mac, who has always been an achiever – a do-er, just like her father. After the death of her mother, she finds that she needs to get away, so she buys a little run-down stone cottage in the middle of nowhere to transform into a creative studio. She is taken by the feel of the place - especially the twisted weeping willow tree behind the house, even though it doesn't fit into her plans anywhere.

Dan spent years growing up on the old Guthrie place, so when the new owner arrives, he is not convinced that he wants to work for this headstrong woman, who is obviously used to getting what she wants, but he feels that it is something he has to do – and only God knows why.

Can Dan and Mac work together to make her dreams into a reality? Will she transform the old Guthrie place, and her life, into something unique and beautiful? And what will become of The Crying Tree?

The Bush Olympics

The Bush Olympics, written by Olwyn Harris and beautifully illustrated by Shelly Askew, shows us that we don't have to be good at everything to be part of a team. Even sleepy Koala is good at something, and if everyone plays their part, we can all be successful together.